**'I don't know where this attraction between us might lead. I don't know what's going to happen when I get back to Paris. But I can tell you I'll be focused on my work, not on seeing how many Parisian women I can date.'**

'I just thought that now that you've...you know, sort of broken your drought and started enjoying a relationship with me...when you went back—' She stopped and closed her eyes. 'I sound ridiculous.'

'No. No, you don't,' he insisted. 'I'm as much out of my depth as you are, but what I do know is that right here, right now, being with you, I'm happy. I won't make empty promises to you because at the moment my future's in limbo. I don't know what's going to happen once the Fellowship's over, once I get back to my apartment, my work, my life in Paris.'

He looked away from her for a moment but she'd clearly seen the confusion in his eyes.

'I won't bring my uncertainty into your world, Bergan, especially when you've experienced so much uncertainty for most of your life. All I am certain of, at the moment, is that being with you makes me happy, and I haven't felt truly happy in a very long time.'

**Dear Reader**

Welcome to the second book in my *Sunshine General Hospital* series. I love writing stories about friends, and these four women—Mackenzie, Bergan, Sunainah and Reggie—are all interesting and unique in their own ways.

Bergan was probably the most closed-off out of the four women, and it has been both a pleasure and a challenge to help her to open up, to learn how to trust and to accept that there is a man out there who is perfect for her, who doesn't care about her past and who is willing to share a beautiful future with her.

Richard… Oh, what can I say about Richard other than I was completely besotted by him from the moment he entered my imagination? I had a much clearer picture of him than I had of Bergan, when most of the time it's the other way around. I loved his quiet strength, his acceptance of Bergan's past and the realisation that even after heartbreak there can still be a happily-ever-after.

I do hope you enjoy Bergan's and Richard's story—don't forget to find me online and tell me what you think. Go to www.lucyclark.net, where you can find the links to connect with me on both Facebook and Twitter.

Warmest regards

*Lucy*

# RESISTING THE NEW DOC IN TOWN

BY

LUCY CLARK

All the characters in this book have no existence outside the imagination of the author, and have no relation whatsoever to anyone bearing the same name or names. They are not even distantly inspired by any individual known or unknown to the author, and all the incidents are pure invention.



First published in Great Britain 2013
by Mills & Boon, an imprint of Harlequin (UK) Limited.
Harlequin (UK) Limited, Eton House, 18-24 Paradise Road,
Richmond, Surrey TW9 1SR



ISBN: 978 0 263 23534 0



ɛnewable
ustainable
to the

**Lucy Clark** is actually a husband-and-wife writing team. They enjoy taking holidays with their children, during which they discuss and develop new ideas for their books using the fantastic Australian scenery. They use their daily walks to talk over characterisation and fine details of the wonderful stories they produce, and are avid movie buffs. They live on the edge of a popular wine district in South Australia with their two children, and enjoy spending family time together at weekends.

**Recent titles by Lucy Clark:**

ONE LIFE-CHANGING MOMENT
DARE SHE DREAM OF FOREVER?
A SOCIALITE'S CHRISTMAS WISH
FALLING FOR DR FEARLESS
DIAMOND RING FOR THE ICE QUEEN
THE BOSS SHE CAN'T RESIST
WEDDING ON THE BABY WARD
SPECIAL CARE BABY MIRACLE

**These books are also available in eBook format from www.millsandboon.co.uk**

To my big sister Kate.

From the moment I was born you have been there for me,
a never-failing tower of strength.

Thanks, sis.

Psalm 91:2-4

# CHAPTER ONE

THIS WAS ONE of the many times Richard Allington was pleased he was six feet five inches tall. In an effort to stay awake and combat jet lag, he'd taken up his mother's suggestion and come to Maroochydore's annual Moon Lantern festival, but now, as he stood in a crowd of thousands upon thousands of people, he wondered if he'd made the right decision.

There were so many people, jostling to get here or there, calling out to their friends, waving or just shoving past without a care. Many different languages were spoken, but thanks to his travels he found himself able to understand the odd word in Mandarin or Japanese as people continued to shove past him. Up on the huge open stage, with its large flat screens on either side, was the last dance act, a group of young Indian women, dancing in colourful saris.

Richard clapped with the rest of the crowd as the women finished and left the stage, and the master of ceremonies came on to announce that with the full moon now rising in the night sky, the extensive lantern festival would soon begin.

Smothering a yawn, Richard moved through the crowd towards the stage, interested to see just what some of these 'lanterns' actually looked like. He could well imagine they'd be nothing like the lanterns Miss Florence Nightingale would have carried around hospital wards.

From what he could see, the lanterns were all at least over two metres high. So far, he'd seen one in the shape of a tiger, one in the form of a bee buzzing around a honey pot and another made to resemble an old yellow taxi. He'd read a sign earlier explaining that the lanterns were all made with balsa wood frames then covered with tissue paper and decorated. It certainly sounded like a skilled operation and Richard could well appreciate the time and effort people had put into making these lanterns.

'I don't want to do it!' The loud, vehement words cut through the crowd and a few people turned to see what the commotion was all about. Richard was one of them, and as he shifted closer to where the young male voice had come from, he saw a heavily tattooed and pierced teenager, dressed from head to toe in black clothing, glaring fiercely at the woman before him.

He was standing in a group with about twenty other young teens, all dressed similarly in dark clothes, congregating in the lantern marshalling area, waiting to take their turn in carrying the amazingly structured lantern next to them. The young man, who Richard guessed to be about sixteen or seventeen years old, had his arms crossed defiantly over his chest, towering by a few inches over the woman who was talking to him with assured calmness.

Richard couldn't help but stare at her, captivated not only with the way she was handling the teenage tantrum with amazing alacrity but also by her beauty. She couldn't be more than about five foot six, slim with a long auburn plait swishing down her back as she moved her head. She was dressed in flat, black boots, denim jeans and a white top. Neat, casual, classic.

Although he had no idea what had initially caused the

young man to flip out, Richard couldn't help but admire the way the woman had instantly taken charge of the situation, defusing what might have resulted in a teenage, ticking time bomb.

Some of the other kids were trying their best not to listen, but others were clearly supporting the woman, agreeing with her. A few of them pointed to the two-metre-high lantern they were about to carry along the snaking path that wound its way through the large crowd. Richard looked away from the woman for a moment to look at the lantern. The words 'Maroochydore Drop-In Centre' had been printed carefully on the side. He instantly looked back to the woman. Was she a social worker of some kind?

He couldn't help but edge closer, not necessarily wanting to hear what the woman was saying to the young man, more intrigued to know what her voice sounded like. Was it as beautiful as her face? As calm as her attitude? He shuffled his way through the crowd and was soon closer than before.

'You've put so much work into this lantern, Drak.' Her smooth, clear tones floated through the air towards him. 'I think it's important for you to carry it in the parade.' There was no sarcasm or censure in her tone, but there was a lot of pride. 'It's not a bad thing to take pride in something you've made. And I'll tell you another thing…' Her smile was small but earnest. 'Now that I know just how talented you really are, I'm not going to let you hide this gift anymore. I have big plans for you, my friend.' Her encouraging smile grew bigger as Drak groaned and shook his head, but Richard could see that he was almost puffing out his chest with pride at her words, and his arms weren't folded nearly as tightly as before.

'I knew this lantern thing was a mistake.' Drak's tone was gruff but not stern. 'It's going to be embarrassing, carrying it.'

'Nah. You can do it, Drak. You're awesome,' a teenage girl about the same age as Drak said encouragingly.

'Jammo's right, Drak. You see an embarrassment. I see brilliance. It's all just a matter of perspective. Also, I'll bet there are oodles of people here tonight who would love to have your gift of being able to create such a thing of beauty.'

'You think it's beautiful?' Drak asked, looking quizzically at the lantern.

'Undoubtedly. And so will many other people. They won't think it's sissy or girly to be able to create something like this. They'll think it's clever, skilful and…magical.'

He gave her a sceptical glance. 'Magical?'

The woman smiled. 'So you'll help carry it? Please?' She didn't break eye contact with Drak, the glow of the drop-in centre's lantern giving her a sort of angelic halo as she waited for his answer.

'Fine, Bergan. I'll carry it.'

'Thank you.'

'Bergan.' Richard found himself whispering her unusual name. Then he frowned for a moment, realising he'd heard that name somewhere else, somewhere before tonight, but right now his brain was still too jet-lagged to figure it out. As though she'd heard him whisper her name, as though he was almost willing her to look his way, Bergan patted Drak on the shoulder, then actually glanced his way, staring directly at him, her honey-brown eyes still bright from her triumph.

Their gazes locked for what seemed an eternity, yet in reality was only about five seconds. She raised an eyebrow, as though asking him what he thought of the situation. But that couldn't possibly have been what that look had meant. They didn't even know each other—why would she be interested in his opinion? And why, as he continued to watch her encouraging Drak, had his mouth gone dry and his gut feel as though it had been tied in knots? Who *was* this woman?

Just then, Richard saw one of the organisers come up to Bergan and speak to her. She listened, nodded, then turned to face the group of teenagers.

'All right. We're up next. Get ready to go,' she called. Richard continued to be amazed at the way she expertly organised everyone, talking to a few of the other adults who were no doubt her colleagues at the drop-in centre. Within another three minutes the people of the Maroochydore Drop-In Centre were ready to show their lantern to the thousands of people gathered for the festival.

Richard watched for as long as he could as Bergan and her crew snaked their way up the hill, with Drak and his mates carrying the lantern, which was shaped like a house with its doors wide open. The young man was indeed very talented to have made such a thing. Finally, when they had delivered their lantern to the top of the hill, where it was placed with the other lanterns on display, the members of the drop-in centre disappeared into the crowd. Where had Bergan gone?

Even once the festivities were finished and people began to disperse and head home, Richard found himself loitering, unable to admit to himself he was waiting for just one more glimpse of Bergan, the gorgeous brown-eyed redhead who had clearly made a difference in a young man's life tonight. He took photographs of all the lanterns on display. He continued to hang around, waiting for the owners of the lanterns to come and remove them, unable to quell his disappointment when a group of teenagers came to collect the drop-in centre's lantern. There was no sign of the beautiful Bergan.

Calling himself foolish, Richard spun on his heel and struck out with the rest of the dwindling crowd, heading towards his car, which he'd had to park at least five blocks away. It had been many, many years since just the sight of a woman had captivated him in such a way. As he pulled into the cul-de-sac where his parents lived, garaged the car and walked into the dark and empty townhouse, he couldn't help but be a little puzzled as to why he'd been so intrigued by a beautiful stranger.

He noticed the light was flashing on his parents' answering machine and listened to the message. It was from his mother, telling him they'd arrived safely in Paris and were now installed in his apartment on Rue de Valance. Richard was glad he'd finally been able to persuade his parents to travel, especially as he was now busy travelling around on an international fellowship, meaning his apartment was sitting empty.

The fellowship not only enabled him to travel, spending time at various accident and emergency departments around the world, but also to gather information on the latest technological and biomedical advancements each country had to offer. Ten countries had been included in the terms of the fellowship, and when Australia had been offered, Richard had requested to do his four-week placement at Sunshine General hospital, mainly because that was the hospital where he'd done his medical training so many years ago.

After Australia, he would return to the northern hemisphere and write up an extensive report of his findings, which would be shared with all the countries he'd visited. After that, he'd return to his job in Paris, working in the public hospital's ER.

Deciding he should probably make himself a late snack, he yawned, hating the fact that he was still jet-lagged from his flight two days ago. He'd forgotten how travelling to the other side of the world could mess with a person's body clock. It was imperative he get a good night's sleep as he was due to start work at Sunshine General tomorrow morning and he doubted the A and E director, who he would be working closely with throughout the duration of his placement, would take kindly to him falling asleep whilst on duty.

Twenty minutes later, at nine-thirty in the evening, he laid his head on the pillow and closed his eyes thankfully, only to be awoken moments later by one of his neighbours coming home, obviously with a carload of happy revellers. It was a Sunday evening, for heaven's sake. Why were they revelling?

He pulled the spare pillow over his head in an attempt to drown out the noise of car doors being closed and friends laughing and chatting with each other. It appeared his neighbours on either side had gone out together, one of them with a very excited child. After ten minutes of chatting and laughing, they called goodnight to one another, and within another few moments the cul-de-sac was quiet once more.

Exhaling with relief, Richard shifted the pillows into a more comfortable position and gratefully drifted off into a deep, deep sleep.

'He's late!' Bergan wasn't happy. As director of the A and E department, she was a stickler for punctuality, and for her new international emergency travelling fellow to be late for his first shift didn't make for a good impression at all. She knew his name. Richard Allington. She knew his parents, Helen and Thomas, as they'd been her neighbours for the past few years in the small cul-de-sac of four townhouses. Now his parents had headed overseas and Richard was staying at his parents' house, or at least that's what Helen had told her. That meant Richard was her new neighbour.

She frowned. Having been raised in a foster-home environment, Bergan had learned the hard way the importance of compartmentalising her life. She'd learned how to get along with people she didn't necessarily like, and she'd learned how to ensure the government system, supporting fostered children, worked in her favour.

She'd worked hard, transforming herself from a desperate, abandoned child to an educated woman who now ran a busy A and E department—but one of the rules she'd worked hard to follow was to keep her personal and professional lives as separate as possible. There were exceptions to the rule, of course, especially with her three closest friends, Mackenzie, Reggie and Sunainah, but even then those relationships had taken years to forge.

Bergan checked her watch, her frown deepening as she realised it displayed exactly the same time as the A and E clock on the wall.

'Perhaps you should have knocked on his door this morning and woken him up yourself,' Mackenzie offered as she wrote in a set of case notes.

Bergan stepped closer to Mackenzie, not wanting the A and E nurses working nearby at the desk to overhear their conversation. 'I don't even like it that this new fellow lives next door to me, so why on earth should I assume responsibility for him arriving on time? You know I don't like interacting with my colleagues in a social setting.'

'I live next door to you,' Mackenzie offered, and received a bored stare from Bergan.

'You're different and you know it. You're the closest person I have to family, you nutter.' A small smile teased at Bergan's lips, but only for a moment. 'You know I'd be lost without you and Sunainah and Reggie. I freely admit it. But neither do I work hand in hand with any of you every single day.' The frown returned as she checked her watch once more, clicking her tongue in annoyance.

'True, but at least Richard's only here for four weeks. Then he moves on to the next port of call for his travelling fellowship.' Mackenzie closed the set of case notes and checked her watch, the wedding ring on her left hand gleaming brightly. Married only three months, Bergan had never seen her friend this happy. 'And speaking of moving on, I'm due to start my orthopaedic clinic in exactly three minutes so I'd best get my butt upstairs.'

'Especially before your husband starts calling you to find out where you are,' Bergan added, a small smile on her lips.

Mackenzie shrugged one shoulder, her own smile incredibly bright and happy. 'It's not so bad being married to the boss.' She winked at Bergan and turned to walk out the nurses' station when a loud commotion came from the front doors leading into the A and E department. Together, Bergan and Mackenzie stared as a tall man came bursting through the doors, trying to shove his arms into a white coat, holding the tube of his stethoscope in his mouth as he narrowly avoided a barouche coming the opposite way.

'Sorry,' he mumbled, finally shoving his arm into the right sleeve and shrugging the coat onto his broad shoulders. Next, he looped the stethoscope around his shoulders, fixed his shirt collar and straightened his striped tie. He paused for a split second, taking in his surroundings, before heading with purposeful strides towards the nurses' station.

It wasn't until he was three steps away from where Bergan stood that he saw her. He stopped stock still and openly gaped, his eyebrows raised in astonishment. 'It's you!'

'What's that supposed to mean?' she retorted, glaring at him with impatience. 'Of course it's me, Dr Allington.'

He blinked one long blink, then stared at her in disbelief. 'You know who I am?'

Bergan shot Mackenzie a look as if to say, 'can you believe this guy?' Mackenzie instantly smiled before holding out her hand.

'Hi. I'm Mackenzie. I live in number two.' She briefly shook hands with him before jerking her thumb over her shoulder. 'Bergan's in number four and while I'd love to hang around and chat, I'm late for clinic. Look forward to catching up with you later, Richard.' And with that, Mackenzie headed off towards the orthopaedic department, leaving Bergan and Richard just standing there, staring at each other.

'What did she mean?' Completely puzzled, Richard eventually found his voice, desperately trying to clear his still jet-lagged mind in order to try and make some sense of what was happening. 'You live in number four?'

Bergan rolled her eyes and clenched her jaw, not wanting to have this discussion in the middle of the nurses' station where she knew several of the staff were sneaking interested glances their way. She couldn't blame them. Richard Allington had arrived at Sunshine General Hospital's A and E department with a crash, boom, bang. Add to that the fact that he was extremely good looking with his tall, dark and handsome stature and eyes of the bluest blue, and she could well imagine why the female staff were willing to stand around ogling their new colleague instead of tending to their duties.

She also had no idea why she'd mentally catalogued his features. Usually, she thought of her colleagues in terms of their abilities rather than their looks, but as she continued to stare at Richard for another moment, recalling the photographs she'd seen of him hanging on the walls at his parents' place, she realised those pictures hadn't done justice to those incredible eyes of his. Was he wearing contacts? Was that why they were so perfectly blue?

She gave her head a little shake, desperate to clear it of such thoughts. She couldn't remember the last time she'd stood and stared at a man like this, feeling a flurry of excitement churning in her belly. He was a colleague, for heaven's sake! How could she be so unprofessional? Forcing herself to look away, she cleared her throat and made sure her tone was crisp and impersonal. 'Dr Allington. If you'd be so kind as to step into my office, we'll tidy up the remaining paperwork so you can legally start your first shift.'

The words had been polite enough, but they'd been said through gritted teeth and as Bergan stalked out of the nurses' station, an intrigued Richard followed closely behind. How was it possible that the one woman he'd noticed at the Moon Lantern festival, that one woman out of hundreds of thousands of people, was now leading him down a small corridor in the A and E department towards her office?

He'd even dreamed of her last night, dreamed he was back at the festival and that after she'd finished talking to her teenage charge, she'd lifted her gaze to meet his once more and had smiled sweetly at him. He'd returned her smile and, after a long moment, she'd quickly excused herself from the throng of teenagers and made her way over to where he was standing, looking as though she had every intention of striking up a conversation.

'You handled that very well,' he'd complimented her. 'Very diplomatic.'

'Thanks. Listen, I have a...thing to do,' she'd said, jerking a perfectly manicured thumb over her shoulder towards the group of teens waiting to take part in the festival. 'But afterwards how about we meet up right back here and, well...?' She'd shrugged a perfectly elegant shoulder and then smiled a perfectly suggestive smile at him. 'Have a cup of coffee or something?'

Richard shook his head, bringing his thoughts back to the present. The dream had been nothing more than a dream. This was reality, and Bergan had stopped in front of an office door. The problem was that he'd been so caught up in his reverie that he'd almost collided with her. He stopped short and quickly took a step back, just as she glanced at him over her shoulder and gave him a perfectly annoyed look. Shaking her head, she used the pass card hanging around her neck on a hospital lanyard to unlock the door, then headed inside the brightly lit office.

As Richard entered the room, he read the name plate: *'Bergan Moncrief. Director'.*

'Bergan Moncrief?' He spoke out loud. 'That's your name?'

She walked behind her desk and waved a hand towards the door. 'That's what it says. Why? Who did you think I was?' She waited for him to speak, but when he didn't say anything immediately, she spread her hands wide. 'Didn't it state my name on your paperwork? I'm not really sure how your travelling fellowship works, but I would have thought you at least have a contact person at each different hospital. Right?'

'Bergan Moncrief.' He stated her name again, the penny finally starting to drop. He *had* heard that name before and it had been his mother who had mentioned it. Bergan Moncrief. Yes. He remembered now. 'You live next door to my paren—' He stopped and nodded as realisation dawned. 'So *that's* what Mackenzie meant. She's at number two, you're at number four and my parents live at number three.'

It was Bergan's turn to show her puzzlement. 'I thought your mother told you.'

'Told me what?'

'That you'd be working with me here at the hospital.' She spread her hands wide, her smile polite, official. 'She certainly mentioned it to me, on more than one occasion, and asked me to make you feel welcome. So…I guess…welcome.'

'I do remember her saying something about knowing some of the people I'd be working with, but she told me that before my fellowship started, which was almost a year ago.' Richard came farther into the room and dropped comfortably into the chair opposite her desk, glad to finally be on the same page as the beautiful Bergan. 'I'm still rather jet-lagged. Even after all the travelling I've done, and even though I try to sleep on the planes and keep myself hydrated and all the other things you're supposed to do to combat jet lag, they haven't worked.'

He watched as Bergan slowly lowered herself into her chair, back still straight, mind on alert, as though she didn't trust him one little bit. And why should she? They knew next to nothing about each other, and yet Richard couldn't help but feel that the brief glance they'd shared at the festival had penetrated them both deeper than they'd like to admit.

'I hope that's not going to interfere with your work today.' Her words were brisk. 'You've already turned up late.'

'I'd like to apologise for that. For some reason, my alarm didn't go off or else I slept right through it.' He scratched his head, as though completely baffled by the situation. There was a small, lopsided smile tugging at the corner of his mouth and as he held her gaze, she once more found herself staring into his gorgeous eyes. He *was* cute. That wasn't up for debate, but her reaction to him was, and once more she had to force herself to look away.

'Hmm.' Bergan continued to frown as she shuffled some papers around on her desk until she found the manila folder she was looking for. She sounded completely uninterested in what he was saying. Richard wasn't sure whether to be happy she wasn't going to belabour the point or sad because she'd dismissed his explanation so easily. He didn't know why he wanted more of her attention. For some reason, this woman intrigued him and right now he wanted to see the same smile on her lips as she'd had last night at the lantern festival.

'Not only did I sleep through my alarm,' he continued, while she prepared the papers in front of her, 'but I was plagued last night with some very noisy neighbours, chatting not too far from my open bedroom window at some ridiculous hour.' There was a teasing note in his tone, but instead of getting her to smile, he watched as she glared at him, bristling with annoyance.

'It wasn't *that* late. And as I saw you at the festival, you can't possibly have been in bed all that long by the time we arrived home. And, yes, we probably shouldn't have chatted so loudly, but Ruthie was excited as she's never been to a Moon Lantern festival before and—'

'Whoa. Whoa.' He held up his hands in a defensive manner, chuckling lightly. 'I was only teasing.'

Bergan closed her open mouth and frowned, desperate to ignore the glorious sound of his deep laughter, which had momentarily filled her office. The only way she knew how to deal with this situation was to be blunt with him. Perhaps, once he knew where she stood, they could begin their professional relationship and put an end to his silly teasing.

'Then don't. I think I should let you know right from the start that I don't particularly like mixing business with pleasure. In other words, I don't like the people I work with on a daily basis knowing too much about my private life. I am the director of a very busy department and as such demand a certain level of respect from my colleagues and staff. The fact that you are my neighbour means I'll be asking you to respect those boundaries. If we happen to see each other around the cul-de-sac, that's one thing, but I will not have you chatting or gossiping about my private life with anyone here at the hospital. Is that clear?'

'Crystal.' He nodded then paused, a thoughtful look on his face, but when he spoke, that same teasing note was still evident in his tone. 'What about Mackenzie? She's your neighbour and now she's my neighbour, so am I allowed to discuss cul-de-sac goings-on with her within hospital grounds?'

Bergan sighed heavily and rolled her eyes, shaking her head. 'Does your mother know how annoying you can be? Because she never said anything about it to me.'

Where she'd intended her words to be a bit of chastisement, to help bring him back into line, she was surprised when Richard stared at her for a split second before throwing his head back and laughing. The warm, rich sound washed over her like a comforting memory and Bergan was slightly confused to how she could be both annoyed and attracted to him at the same time.

There was no denying he was a good-looking man. The phrase tall, dark and handsome fit Richard Allington to perfection, but she'd never been the type of person to judge someone simply on looks. His relaxed, teasing demeanour, on the other hand, was certainly reason enough for her to remember to keep a professional distance from him at all times.

'I'm fairly sure Mum knows. So do my sisters. That's what big brothers do, they annoy their sisters.'

Forcing herself to look away from his dazzling blue eyes, especially as they were twinkling with mirth, Bergan decided it was better not to give him any more reasons to tease her and pushed the manila folder towards him, along with a pen.

'Well, as I am not your sister, would you kindly refrain and concentrate on your job? Now, if you would read these documents and sign them, I can issue you with your pass card. Then you'll need to head down to Personnel to have your photograph taken for your identification badge. Once that's done, report back to me and we'll sign the last lot of papers. Then you'll be all cleared to work at Sunshine General for the next four weeks of your travelling fellowship.'

'You say those words with such disdain.' Richard leaned forward in his chair, that infuriating smile still in place. 'You don't want me here, do you?' he asked.

'What I want, Dr Allington—'

'Richard, please,' he interrupted. 'After all, we *are* neighbours.'

Bergan gritted her teeth. Had he heard nothing of what she'd said? Was he intent on thwarting her by not adhering to her wishes to keep her professional and private lives separate?

'As I was saying, *Richard*,' she replied pointedly, 'what I want is to keep my department functioning as smoothly and as efficiently as it always has. Whether you're going to be a help or a hindrance is yet to be seen, and with the way you all but burst through the front doors this morning, and have hardly been serious since your arrival, I'm inclined to believe it's the latter.'

Richard chuckled at her words as he took the folder and started scanning the pages. 'Fair point. Looks as though I'll have my work cut out for me in changing your mind.'

She hoped he wouldn't, but instead of prolonging the conversation, Bergan nodded towards the documents he was holding, clearly wanting to be done with this interview. When the phone on her desk shrilled to life, she picked it up instantly. 'Dr Moncrief.' She listened for a moment before saying, 'I'll be right there,' and returning the receiver to its cradle.

'Problem?' Richard asked as he finished signing the documents, watching as Bergan rose from her chair with poise and grace. She flicked the long auburn braid from her shoulder and lifted her chin just a touch. The action caused something to tighten deep within his gut and Richard couldn't help but accept the fact that he was indeed attracted to this woman who appeared to want as little to do with him as possible.

'Multiple MVA.'

'Ambulance ETA?'

'Five minutes.'

'Right.' He quickly rose to his feet, his entire demeanour changing so quickly that Bergan was momentarily stunned. 'Let's go, then.' Within two of his long strides he was at her door and holding it open for her to precede him.

'But the paperwork—' She came round her desk. She'd hoped to send him off to Personnel while she went to deal with the emergency, but with the way he'd changed from being all teasing and jovial to the stern medical professional now standing by her open door, she wasn't sure how to react.

'The important forms have all been signed, so the hospital's public liability and my personal insurance are all in order.' He followed her out of her office and checked the door was locked behind them, before heading down the corridor. 'How would you like to handle this? You take trauma room one and I'll take trauma room two, or would you prefer to assess my capabilities and confirm I really do have the extensive qualifications listed on my curriculum vitae?'

As they re-entered the bustling accident and emergency department, they found a hive of activity. Nurses, registrars and interns were all ensuring stock and treatment rooms were ready and waiting for when the first lot of patients started arriving.

'Bergan?'

She glanced up at Richard, who was clearly waiting for her response. She had read his CV and his qualifications were indeed extensive, more so than her own. Initially she had planned to monitor him, to reassure herself of his abilities, but now, with no other qualified A and E consultants presently on the floor, it would be beneficial to have him running one trauma room while she ran the other. Trust. That's what it came down to and Bergan was not the type of woman to trust easily. Not at all.

'I'm happy either way,' he said, prompting her a little. 'It's your call.'

The sound of ambulance sirens was drawing nearer, almost at the hospital gates, and some of the staff were heading out to meet the ambulances. She glanced around at the registrars on duty, the experienced nurses, and knew that a wise director would use the resources presently available to her.

Swallowing, she returned her gaze to meet Richard's and nodded. 'As you said, I'll take trauma room one, you take trauma room two.'

'Thanks for the trust.' He nodded, a small, knowing smile touching his lips as though he'd enjoyed watching her thought processes at work. 'See you on the other side.' And with that he spun on his heel and headed off in the direction of trauma room two, but not before turning to look at her over his shoulder and giving her a cheeky wink.

It was the wink that did it. Bergan had been fine until then, holding herself under control in the presence of the man who not only riled her but also had the ability to set her entire body tingling with one of his infuriating smiles and warm laughter. The cheeky wink was worse, as she felt her knees weaken, her mouth go dry and her head spin. Why would such a handsome, intelligent man choose *her* to flirt with? And at such a moment as this! She reached out a hand towards the wall in an effort to steady herself, hating the feeling of being so unbalanced.

When she'd seen him at the Moon Lantern festival, she'd instantly recognised him from the family photographs his mother, Helen, had on display around on the walls of her home. Bergan had been surprised, first, at just how tall he was in the flesh and, second, that from one brief, momentary glance she'd been hit with the same sensations she was experiencing now.

Never before had a man been able to make her almost swoon with just a look, or a smile, or a wink. No one... except, it appeared, Richard Allington. And the most annoying thing was that he'd done it twice.

As she dragged in a breath and stood up straight, squaring her shoulders and preparing her mind for the busy task ahead, Bergan was determined that although her new colleague may have cause havoc with her equilibrium, she would force herself to be immune to him. She was a strong, independent woman who had worked hard for many years to gain control over her silly, schoolgirl emotions.

Yes, she would be immune to him, she thought as she pushed away the emotions he'd evoked. And that was most definitely that.

# CHAPTER TWO

IN A AND E, BERGAN remained the focused and consummate professional that she'd worked so hard to become. It certainly wasn't every day that a man could enter her well-ordered, neat and controlled world and make her knees weaken with a single smile, and for that reason alone she knew she needed to keep her distance from Richard Allington.

The fact that she was friends with his parents, and that for the next four weeks he would be her neighbour as well as working alongside her at the hospital, meant that it was going to be difficult to maintain her composure, but she'd lived through much tougher situations than this and she'd always come out on top.

*It's only four weeks*, she'd thought over and over again, every time she'd caught a glimpse of him roaming around *her* A and E, tending to patients, chatting with staff, flirting with every available female. He was just the same as every other man, interested in only one thing—conquering and controlling a woman. Well, she certainly wasn't going to fall for his charm and charisma.

Having been raised in foster homes since she'd been small, her parents both drug addicts, Bergan had grown up with a skin much tougher than that of the average little girl. Bad things had happened to her and she'd forged her own way through them, coming out stronger and more determined than ever. Now, after many years of hard work, she was the director of a busy A and E department, running it effectively and efficiently, respected by her colleagues and peers. Four weeks wasn't long. She could and *would* survive the onslaught to her life that *was* Richard Allington.

Squaring her shoulders, she headed to the nurses' station, where he was leaning comfortably against the desk, chatting with Katrina, one of the best retrieval and triage nurses Bergan had ever worked with. 'All done?' Bergan asked, barely glancing in his direction as she sat down to write up a set of case notes.

'Basically.' There was a hint of relief combined with satisfaction in Richard's voice. 'Just waiting for two patients to return from Radiology, but the most serious cases are off and away to Theatres.'

'Off and away?' Bergan looked up at him, unable to stop the small smile tugging at the corners of her mouth. 'You do realise you said those words with a hint of an Irish accent?' she pointed out.

'No, I didn't.' Richard shifted from the desk and shoved one hand into the pocket of his trousers. 'Did I?'

'You did,' Katrina confirmed for him, smiling brightly at the handsome doctor. 'Have you worked in Ireland?'

'A few months ago, yes, but I hadn't realised I'd picked up any of the accent.' He shrugged one shoulder, his smile brightening. 'One problem I have had during this fellowship has been to control my French—and I mean that literally. Having lived and worked in France for the past six years, for the first few months of the fellowship, when I was in emergency situations, as we were just now, I'd often break into rapid French when giving instructions to staff. It was only when they all stopped and stared at me as though I'd grown an extra head that I even realised I'd done it.' He chuckled and Katrina joined in.

Bergan's smile increased as she pictured the stunned looks on people's faces at an Australian doctor, working in somewhere like Spain, giving out instructions in French. Then, as though realising she was enjoying his company, she quickly frowned and returned her attention to the case notes open in front of her.

'What led you to settle in France in the first place?' It was Katrina who had asked the question, but Bergan was very interested in the answer. Although she'd known Richard's parents for quite a few years now, it wasn't as though they all sat around listening to Helen's anecdotes about her children's accomplishments. And at any rate Bergan preferred not to engage in deeply personal conversations with people, except for her three closest friends, who had definitely proved themselves worthy of her friendship over the many years they'd been together.

Would Richard prove himself worthy? The question jumped into her head unbidden and she quickly shook it away. Her friendships with Sunainah and Reggie had been forged well over a decade ago and Mackenzie was the closest thing she had to a sibling, as they had both been raised in the foster system. Richard was here for one month and she doubted if that was long enough for any man, no matter how ambitious, to break through the barriers she'd spent almost a lifetime putting carefully in place.

Even though she was writing in the case notes, Bergan couldn't help but listen to his reply to Katrina's question.

'It was one of those strange things that happened. I was working in the UK, my contract about to expire, and a friend who worked at the public hospital in Paris told me of a job going there. Well, I spoke the language so I thought—why not?' He shrugged nonchalantly and yet… Bergan could have sworn she heard something in his tone that suggested there was much more to the story than he was telling.

She glanced up at him, quickly noting that his previously jovial blue eyes now reflected a hint of sadness.

'And one year morphed into two years then three, and before I knew it I'd been working at the hospital for six years.'

'And then you were offered the fellowship?' Katrina asked.

'That's right. My first two years in Paris…I actually worked part time and did some further study, which meant I was qualified for the fellowship.'

There it was again, Bergan thought. That little pause in his words, as though he was choosing them carefully. Was he avoiding saying something too personal? Perhaps the cheeky, arrogant man she'd met earlier that morning wasn't all there was to Richard Allington.

'Well,' he said a moment later, drawing in a long breath and slowly exhaling, 'I don't know about you, but three hours of dealing with emergencies has left me with an appetite. Care to join me?'

Bergan kept writing up the notes, thinking he was talking to Katrina, but it wasn't until the nurse cleared her throat that Bergan looked at her. Katrina nodded pointedly in Richard's direction and it was only then Bergan realised he'd been talking to *her*. 'Oh!' She stared at him for a moment, his words sinking in. 'You're asking me to join you for a late lunch?'

Richard watched her closely for several seconds before replying. 'I'm asking if you wouldn't mind accompanying me to the hospital cafeteria so we can continue our debriefing.' He spread his hands wide. 'I'm hungry. You've got to be hungry, too, and it just seems to make sense if we eat and get some work accomplished at the same time.'

'Go, Bergan,' Katrina encouraged. 'I can follow up with the patients who are in Radiology if they come back before you return.'

Bergan looked at the clock and then, as if on cue, felt her stomach grumble. Her eyes widened and she looked up at Richard, wondering if he'd heard that. His answer was to wink at her again and the same flood of tingles spread through her at the action. At least this time she was sitting down. Why did he have to be so…personable?

She shook her head and forced herself to look back at the case notes before her. Knowing it would probably raise more questions if she declined his polite offer, and as she was clearly hungry, it seemed easier to accept, but still, something held her back from saying so. Probably her strong self-preservation instinct. Already, in just a few short hours, he'd somehow managed to get under her skin and she didn't like it one little bit.

'Is that a no?' he asked, as she signed the case notes and handed them to Katrina, who instantly took them from her, mumbled an excuse of some sort and left them alone.

'What?'

'You shook your head. Does that mean you don't want us to eat together?'

'I don't really have anything else to debrief you on. There are just a few more forms to sign, but…'

Richard shifted his stance and gave her a look of veiled amusement, as though he could easily read her thoughts and knew she didn't want to spend time with him. 'Well, I'm not up to date with mine. I have several forms that require your signature.' He held out a hand towards her, but Bergan ignored it, rising to her feet and pushing in the chair. 'It's business, Bergan. Two colleagues walking together, eating together. Nothing more sinister than that, I promise.'

Bergan sighed heavily, knowing if she kept refusing him

he might end up making a mountain out of a molehill. After all, he was an international fellow, and for Sunshine General to host such an accomplished doctor as Richard Allington had been quite a coup. 'Fine,' she said, rolling her eyes. The action, designed to show her impatience and to let him know once and for all that she wasn't happy with this arrangement, brought an unexpected chuckle from him.

'Thank you. You do me a great honour.'

She ignored the way his light laughter washed over her, ignored the delighted prickling down her spine, which heightened her awareness of him. 'You're teasing me,' she murmured as she headed out of A and E, catching Katrina's gaze and mouthing the word 'Lunch'.

He chuckled again as they entered the stairwell, the rich, deep sound echoing around the walls. Bergan tried not to like the way his laughter made her feel. It had been a long time since any man had dared to tease her. Most of the men she knew were colleagues and although her friend Reggie had done her best to set Bergan up on a few dates, none of the men had interested her.

*'Moi?'* Richard feigned ignorance. 'Tease? *Je ne sais pas ce que vous dites.*'

Bergan was glad she was a few steps in front of him so he didn't see the small smile on her lips. 'Teasing *and* rude. Speaking in a language a simple girl like me would have absolutely no hope of understanding. Tut-tut, Dr Allington.' She glanced at him over her shoulder as they rounded the landing, heading up another flight. 'This is not a good beginning for you.'

'And yet,' Richard said as he came up beside her, easily overtaking her in order to hold the door open, 'why do I get the distinct impression you understood every word I said?' He gave her a quizzical smile as she came up the final few steps. 'Do you speak French?'

'As I said, a simple girl.'

Richard gave a hoot of laughter and Bergan had to close her eyes for a split second in order to block out the delightful sound. She'd made him laugh. She'd actually teased him back, had said something that had made him laugh. That wasn't something she did every day. She much preferred to keep her distance from her male colleagues and as she walked past him Bergan met his gaze, holding it briefly and doing her best to ignore the way his spicy scent penetrated her senses. She had to admit she was mildly surprised with the way Richard didn't appear to be kow-towing to her like so many other men did and while she found that refreshing, it also made him even more dangerous.

Impersonal. Businesslike. Professional. That was the only way to handle a man like him.

'This way to the cafeteria,' she said, pointing down the long corridor. Before Richard could say another word she headed off, knowing he would fall into step beside her within an instant. She also hoped he'd drop the whole teasing demeanour so they could get their work done, eat some food and then get back to A and E, where she could be sufficiently distracted by work, *not* by Richard's close proximity.

'So…did you enjoy the Moon Lantern festival last night?' he asked.

'What are you doing?'

'What do you mean? I'm making conversation.'

'Here?' Bergan frowned as she glanced up at him. 'Didn't I say that I don't like discussing my personal life at work?' She turned her attention from him and nodded politely at another colleague, who was walking in the opposite direction.

'No one can hear our conversation, Bergan.' He kept his voice low, leaning a little closer to her as he spoke, and she immediately moved away, trying desperately to keep a decent distance between them.

'Yet when you lean in like that and speak in that stage whisper, they'll get the wrong idea.'

'I disagree. Anyone seeing two doctors talking in such a fashion will no doubt think we're discussing a patient.'

'Which should be done in the privacy of an office.'

'We're busy people. Sometimes we don't have time to sit and discuss things in an office. We need to talk and chat and eat and process information along with digesting our food. It's the way doctors are.'

Bergan sighed loudly. 'Is there a point to all of this, or shouldn't I ask?'

'All I'm saying is that no one's going to know what we're discussing so if I want to discuss the Moon Lantern festival and the way our eyes seemed to meet across a crowded... er...crowd, then why can't I?'

Bergan stopped momentarily and looked at him with feigned astonishment. 'Oh, gee! Was that you? I hadn't realised.' She raised an eyebrow then continued towards the cafeteria.

'And now you're teasing me!'

Bergan couldn't help the smile that touched her lips. *'Je ne sais pas ce que vous dires.'*

Richard's warm laughter floated over her, but this time it was more than just his deep chuckle. The sound warmed her through and through, but thankfully it was drowned out as they entered the busy and noisy cafeteria. *'Touché, mademoiselle.'*

'And our eyes didn't "meet across the crowded...er... crowd",' she repeated, emphasising the way he'd used the same word twice. 'You make it sound all clandestine and romantic—which it most definitely wasn't.'

'What was it, then?'

'We were just in each other's line of sight. That's all. Nothing more, nothing less.'

She joined the queue, waiting to be served, acutely aware of Richard standing very close behind her. Bergan couldn't believe how aware she was of him and as she licked her dry lips and tried to appear nonchalant and completely unaffected by the man directly behind her, a woman with short, black, feathered hair, tipped with hot pink highlights, sidled up next to her.

'And just *who* is this dishy, dishy man behind you?' Regina Smith asked, placing one hand around Bergan's shoulders and pointing interestedly towards Richard. 'Is this...*him*?'

Bergan sighed and shook her head in bemused astonishment at Reggie's complete lack of inhibition, but then, that was Reggie. 'Reggie Smith, meet Richard Allington.'

'Helen's boy?'

Bergan smothered a smile at the 'boy' part, but nodded as Reggie dropped her arm and shifted closer to Richard, holding out her hand in greeting. *'Enchantée.'*

Richard dutifully grazed his lips across Reggie's knuckles before releasing her hand. Even though it was only a simple action, even though he was only being polite and even though this was hardly unusual behaviour for Reggie, the happiest and bubbliest person Bergan had ever known, she couldn't ignore the thread of jealousy that ripped through her. It was odd, especially as she barely knew anything about Richard, and didn't really want to.

How was it this man, who had been in her world for such a short period of time, had somehow managed to get under her skin? Bergan advanced in the queue as Reggie chatted away, telling Richard all about the latest developments in the general surgical department.

She was positive Richard was smiling brightly and staring at Reggie with his deep, engaging eyes. She couldn't blame him because most men were instantly besotted by Reggie and her bubbly personality, but when it was their turn to be served at the counter, Bergan was surprised to find Richard highly attentive and insisting on paying for both Reggie's lunch and her own.

'You are such a sweetie,' Reggie said, blowing him a kiss. 'But you know this means that both of you simply must eat lunch with me and I won't take no for an answer.' Reggie pointed to the corridor. 'We'll go down the first lot of stairs and then out into the small courtyard. It's such a beautiful, sunshiny day, it seems such a shame to waste it.'

'Every day's a beautiful day in Queensland,' Bergan grumbled, but neither of them took any notice.

Richard readily agreed. 'It *is* rather noisy in here. Bergan and I won't be able to get any work done.'

'Work! Good heavens,' Reggie persisted, shaking a finger at Bergan. Bergan merely shrugged, trying to find a way to wriggle out of this situation. 'Take a break for once, Bergan.'

'Listen to your friend,' Richard said to Bergan pointedly, falling into step beside her once more as they headed to the closest stairwell.

Bergan hadn't wanted to eat lunch with Richard in the first place and now he had Reggie as a playmate, so perhaps he wouldn't insist she stay. At the thought of Reggie and Richard locked together in a whispered conversation, an awful taste came into the back of her throat. Why should she care if Reggie wanted to get to know Richard better—or vice versa, for that matter? True, Richard was only here for a month, but if Reggie didn't mind getting involved with a man who would up and leave her when it was time for him to return to Paris, then so be it. She didn't care. Honestly, she didn't. So why did the thought leave such an uncomfortable sensation in the pit of her stomach?

Bergan didn't say a word until they were outside, the early afternoon sunlight shining brightly into her eyes. She followed Reggie to the courtyard, where one or two people were just finishing their lunches before departing. They sat at the picnic table, Bergan ensuring she didn't end up sitting next to Richard. At least, with the table between them, it afforded her a bit of distance.

Reggie sat next to Richard, keeping up a steady stream of easy chatter for the first five minutes before her phone rang. Reggie quickly excused herself and took the call. 'Uh…duty calls,' she said, rewrapping her sandwich and shifting out of the bench seat. 'Looks as though my afternoon surgical list *is* going to start on time after all. Morning Theatre was running late,' she stated by way of explanation. 'You two stay here and enjoy the sunshine. Bye-ee.'

'And there goes Reggie,' Bergan stated as her friend disappeared.

'Is she always that bright and bubbly?'

'Always.' Bergan nodded for emphasis, a small smile on her lips. 'Even when she's upset, she's still more bubbly than I am on a good day!'

'And she's one of your closest friends?'

'Why does that surprise you?' Bergan straightened her shoulders. Richard was still chewing and hadn't yet swallowed his mouthful so she took the opportunity to keep on talking. 'Do you think that because we're so different that we wouldn't be friends?'

Richard swallowed. 'That's not what I meant.'

'Then what did you mean? Reggie and I are incredibly similar. We just show our feelings in different ways.'

He looked up at the sky as though hoping the answer to the question might just fall down and hit him on the head.

'I only meant that, as you've already told me, you don't like mixing business with pleasure and, well...Reggie seems to be the epitome of someone who does the opposite. I find it...interesting that you're good friends. That's all.' He held his hands up, indicating he had no other secret agenda.

Bergan started rewrapping her salad roll, as though intending to leave. 'You're not the first person to be surprised that someone as nice as Reggie should be friends with someone like me, who is far too often closed off and brusque.'

'That's not what I meant, Bergan.'

'Reggie is loyal, trustworthy and filled with determination to spread sunshine among everyone she meets, and a lot of the time people take advantage of her generous nature. She's had a tough life, and yet she's still happy and nice, wanting everyone to be as happy as she is. And, yes, that can be exhausting to be around all the time, but there is nothing I wouldn't do for her and vice versa.' When she went to stand, Richard instantly reached out a hand and caught hers in his.

'Wait. Don't go. Please?'

'Richard?' She looked pointedly at her hand, but he didn't let her go.

'We've got off on the wrong foot, Bergan. I apologise if you thought I was insulting your friend or even questioning your friendship with Reggie. It's clear you're very loyal to her and I can also see how people might take advantage of her, but I am not that sort of person. I admire your loyalty to your friendships, but I truly didn't mean any disrespect with my questions.' He held her gaze and she could see the exasperation in his eyes. He shook his head. 'This whole morning, this whole day...it hasn't gone the way it usually goes when I start at a new hospital.'

As she lowered herself back onto the bench seat, appeased by his words, Richard let go of her hand. The instant warmth from his touch had been enough to send shock waves ricocheting throughout her entire body and her knees actually wobbled. Sitting down had been the best option to get him to stop playing havoc with her senses.

His words also made her feel quite contrite. It couldn't be easy for him, having to change hospitals every month, starting afresh with a new set of people. 'How does it usually go?'

'I introduce myself to the head of department in a timely and unhurried fashion. We swap paperwork, discuss schedules and then, if time permits, take a tour of the facilities, not only so I can get my bearings in the A and E department and meet a few staff members, but also to see where I'll often be lecturing, as that's part of my fellowship duties.'

'Sounds...ordered, structured. Nice.' She took a sip of her water. 'So why was today's beginning so different?'

'I can make a load of excuses about alarms not going off, jet-lag and noisy neighbours...' He smiled at the last part. 'But I won't because it doesn't change the fact that I was late. Again, I offer my sincerest apologies.'

'Apology accepted.' Bergan swallowed her mouthful. 'So where's this paperwork I need to look at?'

Richard shrugged and gave her a sly smile. 'Actually, I left it at home.'

'But you said we'd be working over lunch,' she protested.

'We are. We're improving public relations.'

'Is that what we're doing?' She didn't sound as though she believed him and took another bite of her roll.

'Actually...' Richard finished his sandwich and balled up the wrapper before tossing it into a nearby bin '...that's not the *only* reason I wanted to have lunch with you.' He spread his arms wide. 'And I couldn't have picked a better setting. Close to the hospital, pretty trees and shrubs, no people. I should thank Reggie for leading us here, although I'm not sorry she had to leave.'

'It was her plan to leave all along.'

Now it was Richard's turn to frown at her. 'What do you mean?'

Bergan swallowed her mouthful and took a sip of her water. 'Reggie's a born matchmaker. She can't help it. Spreading sunshine to everyone she meets is her mission in life.'

This news also helped Richard to realise why Bergan had been so touchy when Reggie had first left. She would have known that Reggie had dragged them outside simply so the two of them could be alone to talk more freely, and, as he'd already deduced, Bergan didn't seem the type of woman to willingly open herself up to anyone. He nodded, processing these thoughts. 'Is that so? Then I have even more to thank her for.'

'I don't get it.' Bergan ate her last mouthful, frowning at him in confusion. 'I thought you only agreed to come out here so you could spend time with Reggie.'

'No. Not Reggie. You.'

'Me?'

'From the first moment I saw you at the Moon Lantern festival, I've been wanting to ask you out. On a date,' he clarified.

His words so surprised Bergan that she swallowed the wrong way and started to choke. Richard was up from the bench and around to her side of the table like a shot, patting her on the back to ensure nothing was lodged in her windpipe.

Bergan took a sip of water then turned to face him, not too happy when he lowered himself onto the bench seat beside her. 'Sorry, you want to do…what now?'

'Ask you out on a date. Dinner? Tomorrow night?'

Bergan stared at him, unsure what to do or say. Tingles flooded her body and a surprising warmth washed over her. Richard *liked* her? The answer should be instant and of the negative variety, but instead she sat there, actually contemplating what it would be like to go on a date with Richard. He was certainly very handsome so she could well understand the appeal there. He was highly intelligent and that also appealed to her. It wasn't as though she didn't know anything about his past because, thanks to his parents, she did.

'Please say yes,' he whispered, and to her astonishment she found really wanted to.

# CHAPTER THREE

BERGAN REACHED FOR her water and took another sip, gently edging back as she needed a bit of distance from his persuasive presence.

'Um…' She swallowed, coughed once, then forced herself to meet his eyes. She'd been turning men down when they asked her on dates for quite some time and her friends had often joked that she was an expert at freezing people with just one look, but for some reason none of that seemed to matter as she looked into Richard's perfectly blue eyes.

They were eyes that reflected his emotions and even though now they looked eager and earnest, she couldn't wipe the memory of earlier when she'd noticed something akin to pain and sadness there. It was clear there was more to Richard than she'd seen so far, but what would happen if she said yes to his question?

He was only here for one month…but perhaps that was a good thing. There was no way she'd ever get attached to any man within such a short space of time. She was the type of woman who liked to take things slowly…*very* slowly…and the average male was far too impatient to spend the time pandering to her whims. Of course, there was a logical reason why she was the way she was, but ordinarily most men couldn't be bothered to take the time to find out what it was.

As Richard's time was clearly limited, surely that meant

she could go out with him a few times—just as friends—and then wave him goodbye when it was time for him to return to Paris?

Bergan sighed slowly, continuing to look into his handsome face, knowing she could probably spend the rest of the day sitting here, staring at him. He really was a very attractive man, even though he'd teased her. He'd more than made up for it during the emergency and it was clear that intellectually they were on the same wavelength.

She wanted to go. She wanted to say yes to his question, but as a smidgen of logical thought returned, she remembered she was always busy on Tuesday evenings.

'I…' She licked her lips and gently shook her head. 'I can't.'

'Because you won't date colleagues?'

'There is that.'

'Then think of us as neighbours.'

Bergan couldn't help but smile. 'I don't date neighbours either.'

'Then who do you date?' Richard sat back and spread his arms wide.

'I don't.' Bergan shifted uncomfortably on the seat and capped her water bottle, knowing she should put an end to this type of conversation as it couldn't lead anywhere. 'At least, not in the way that normal people date. Usually, I go out with someone Reggie has set me up with—mainly to stop her nagging me—because she keeps telling me I'm going to grow old by myself and she can't even bear to think about me being alone.'

'So I need to go through Reggie to get you to agree?'

She didn't answer him and stood instead. 'We'd better get back.'

Richard was by her side so fast she barely had time to register he'd moved. He placed a hand on her upper arm and carefully turned her to face him. 'Have you been hurt in the past? Because I've been hurt, too.'

'So you think we should console each other?'

Richard shrugged one shoulder and gave her that cute half smile of his, the one that seemed to always churn the newly acquired butterflies in her stomach. What was it about him that she was having such a difficult time resisting?

'That's one idea to run with.' He paused then shook his head. 'Would it help if I said I don't really know anyone here? That although we might call it a "date", it would really be more like two acquaintances hanging out and getting to know each other a bit better. A friendship date. We don't even have to go out to a restaurant or anything like that. Pizza? My place?'

Bergan smiled, for some reason pleased with his charming insistence. *Friendship date?* He really did want to spend time with her...but why? She decided it was best to tread carefully. 'I don't eat pizza.'

'Chinese take-out? Or a lovely curry?'

She tipped her head to the side, her long auburn plait falling down her back. 'I already have plans tomorrow night and the next night and the one after that.'

Richard dropped his hand and shoved it into the pocket of his trousers. 'Are you just saying that to let me down gently or are you serious?'

'Deadly serious.' She turned and started walking back towards the hospital building, binning her rubbish as she went.

'Busy every night.' His tone was thoughtful as though she'd just given him a puzzle he needed to unravel. 'You're either here, working late, finishing up paperwork, or...' He watched her for a moment and Bergan couldn't help but look at him in expectation to see what other reasons he might pull from thin air to guess how she spent her evenings. He snapped his fingers. 'Or you're at the drop-in centre.'

Bergan stopped walking in stunned disbelief. 'How do you know—?'

'About the drop-in centre? I *was* at the Moon Lantern festival, remember?'

'Of course.' She closed her eyes for a moment, unable to believe he had figured things out, before she continued walking.

'It isn't common knowledge?'

'It's not a great secret, but neither do I advertise my involvement.'

'So tomorrow night you'll be at the drop-in centre?'

'Yes.'

'Mind if I tag along?'

That surprised her. 'Do you really want to?'

'I have experience with homeless and troubled teens. Believe it or not, they have them in Paris, too. A couple of us help out providing "no-questions-asked" medical support at a few of the youth centres.'

Bergan looked at him, trying to see whether he was just saying these things in order to impress her, but there was sincerity and truth in his face and mannerisms. 'You can come if you want to. The centre is always looking for volunteers and especially ones who are trained.' They headed into the hospital and walked towards A and E.

'OK. Sounds like a plan. What time?'

'I usually get there around eight o'clock.'

'Great. Why don't I get take-out, we can eat and then head in together? It seems silly to take two cars when we're going and returning to the same place. Save petrol and the environment.'

Bergan couldn't help but smile as she glanced at him.

'Sneaky. Don't think I'm unaware of your fake nonchalance, Dr Allington.'

Richard chuckled as she swiped her security card across the sensor, allowing them access to the A and E department. 'Am I that transparent?' His eyes were twinkling with merriment, but he watched as the smile slowly slid from her face.

'I hope you are.'

'Because you don't take kindly to deception.'

'Not at all.'

'Good to know where I stand, Dr Moncrief. Honesty is the only way to proceed.' Then he touched his fingers to his forehead in a salute before turning on his heel, collecting the manila folder with his paperwork from the nurses' station and heading off towards the corridor that led to Personnel.

Bergan watched him go, taking in his long legs, his firm, straight back and very broad shoulders. She stood there until he disappeared from view, not only because she was completely confused by the way she'd reacted to the man but also because, with the way he'd given her that cheeky grin and corny salute, she was fairly sure she was unable to move her legs.

Tomorrow night she had a date…a date with Richard.

'Have you met Bergan and Mackenzie yet?' Richard's mother, Helen, asked him over the phone.

'Yes. In fact, I'm having dinner with Bergan tonight and then we're heading to the drop-in centre.'

There was silence on the other end of the line, and although he was used to the delay that still sometimes happened on international calls, he knew he'd no doubt just shocked his mother.

'Dinner? As in a date? With Bergan?'

'Don't make a big deal out of it, Mum. Besides, it's more like a friendship date. You know I don't know many people here.'

'Friendship date?' Helen sounded as though she didn't believe him. 'Are you forgetting who you're talking to? I'm your mother, Richard. You can't pull the wool over my eyes, even if we are half a world away. I know your tone of voice, my darling.'

Richard closed his eyes, belatedly wishing he hadn't said anything. 'Bergan's nice, even though she does seem…I don't know, to be wound a little tight.'

'She has every right to be, given what she's been through. Look, Richard, I'm not saying don't spend time with her, just…be careful.'

'For her? Or me?' He opened his eyes and walked to the bedroom, crouching down to look under the bed for his shoes. He'd already ordered their dinner but still needed to drive to the restaurant to pick it up.

'Both, but of course I'm worried about you, darling. I'm your mother. I know how difficult it was for you after Chantelle's death, how it was difficult for you to engage with your colleagues on a social level. I know it's the reason why you accepted the fellowship, not only to travel but to force yourself out of that hole you found yourself in.'

'Don't pull any punches, Mum,' he murmured as he sat on the bed and shook his head. 'I have dated since Chantelle's death.'

'Once or twice in how many years?' Helen asked rhetorically.

'I thought you'd be happy,' Richard countered, thinking of the way he'd been captivated by Bergan from the first moment he'd laid eyes on her. He had no idea what it was about the woman that seemed to intrigue him so much, but not even bothering to find out wasn't an option. It was why he'd been a little insistent with her, wanting to discover just why she'd caught his attention.

'I am, darling. Of course I am, but…Bergan…well, just be careful.'

Richard looked at the clock then groaned. 'I've got to go, Mum. I don't want to be late.' After saying their goodbyes, he rang off, tossing his phone onto the bed before pulling on his shoes. He hadn't expected reticence from his mother and it made him wonder what was in Bergan's past that had made his mother hesitate.

'No time like the present for finding out,' he said out loud as he grabbed his phone and walked through the house, picking up his keys and heading to the door. He was taking steps forward. They might be little steps at first, but forward he was moving.

Bergan couldn't believe how flustered she was as she went through yet another change of clothes, checking her reflection in the mirror, worrying that she might be too overdressed or too underdressed.

'Argh!' She stared at her reflection, looking at the casual skirt that came to just above her knees, a plain top and an old cardigan. 'This is stupid.' She turned and stalked to her dresser, picked up her phone and pressed a pre-set number. 'This is stupid,' she said a moment later when Mackenzie answered the call.

'What's stupid?'

'Me. Richard's going to be here in five minutes with dinner and I've changed my outfit seven times.'

Mackenzie couldn't help but chuckle. 'Calm down. You're only having an informal dinner, it's not as though you're out at a five-star restaurant.'

'It would be better if we were because then at least I'd know what to wear. I don't know whether to wear one thing for dinner and then change before we head to the drop-in centre or whether that's too...girly.' Bergan pulled the cardigan off as she spoke. 'You know me. I'm *not* girly. We used to make fun of girls who used to fuss over themselves before dates,' Bergan growled. 'I never thought I'd turn into one of them.'

'You haven't. I'd love to come and help, but Ruthie's in the bath and John's not home from the hospital yet, so instead let me ask you one question.'

'OK.'

'What do you usually wear to the drop-in centre?'

'Jeans, flats, T-shirt, light jacket if it's a coolish evening.'

'So wear that.'

'If I knew what Richard was bringing for dinner, I'd at least be able to gauge the outfit a bit—'

'What does that matter?' Mackenzie interrupted.

'Because he's lived in Paris for so long. When we were travelling after finishing medical school, you didn't spend much time in Paris, but I did, Kenz. I spent three months living there and, believe me, to the French, clothes are an art, along with cuisine. There were certain rules around even the most casual of dinner dates.'

'Ahh...so that's what has you so flustered, the fact that this is a *date*. Now it all makes sense.'

'It's not a date date. It's a friendship date.'

'What's that supposed to mean?'

'I don't know!'

Bergan shook her head and slumped down onto her bed, lying across the large pile of discarded clothes and not caring. 'I haven't been on any sort of date in a very long time, Kenz. You know why.'

'I do, and I think you're incredibly brave, Bergan. In accepting this as a *date*, you're refusing to tar all men with the same brush and that's a big step forward.'

Bergan closed her eyes. 'Even though it was so long ago, it still—'

'I know. You've come so far and you're so brave and you do amazing work at the drop-in centre because you know exactly where those kids are coming from. Focus on that, and the fact that Richard wants to help.'

'He did seem keen.'

'All you're doing is putting food into your stomachs before you go out to help others.'

Bergan opened her eyes and sat up, nodding. 'You're right.'

'Of course I am.'

'What am I fussing about?'

'I have no idea.'

'It's a date…between friends.'

'No reason to stress,' Mackenzie agreed.

'Then why can I hear that smile in your words?' Bergan shook her head. 'You're loving this, aren't you?'

'All I can say is—it happens to the best of us.'

'What does that mea—?' The doorbell downstairs sounded and Bergan jumped up from the bed. 'He's here. *He's here!*'

'Then go.'

'Yes. Good. OK. Love you. 'Bye.' Bergan disconnected the call and quickly reached for her usual jeans and T-shirt combo, pulling them on in a hurried rush, before shoving her feet into a pair of black flats. She glanced once at her reflection, realising her loose hair was a tangled mess, and quickly pulled her fingers through the auburn locks as she raced down the stairs.

'Ow,' she said a moment before opening the front door.

'Are you all right?' Richard asked as he stepped into the house, two brown paper bags filled with containers in his arms. Bergan closed the door behind him.

'Just knots in my hair,' she offered by way of explanation. 'A common problem. Come on through. Something smells good.'

Richard found he was having trouble moving as he stared at the glorious sight of the woman before him. Dressed casually and yet comfortably, she looked so different from the professional woman he'd worked alongside for the past two days, but he had to admit it was her long, glorious auburn locks that had made his mouth go dry and his brain refuse to function.

Now that it was loose, it was far longer than he'd realised, reaching almost to her waist, the colour vibrant and shiny. He wanted nothing more than to reach out his hand and run his fingers through the silky locks, letting them sift through his hand with a tingling delight.

'Richard?'

He forced himself to blink, to move, to do something as he belatedly realised he was just standing there, holding bags of food and staring at her.

'Sorry.' He followed her towards the dining room, where she'd set a basic table. As she walked, he noted the way her hair swished from side to side, a variety of colours—golds, reds and oranges—picked up by the overhead ceiling lights. 'Wow.' The whispered word was ripped from him before he could stop it.

'What?' She looked at the dining table then back at him, her eyes widening as she realised he was staring at *her*.

Richard shook his head. He was behaving like an adolescent schoolboy. He quickly placed the bags of food on the table and crossed his arms over his chest. 'You look… amazing.'

Bergan looked down at the plain and simple clothes she was wearing. 'Really?'

'Uh…' He pointed at her, indicating her hair, feeling

more and more like a stunned idiot with each passing second. 'I haven't seen your hair loose before.' Richard cleared his throat. 'It's... Wow.'

'Oh.' She instantly ran her fingers through the tresses, finding a few more knots, but unable to believe how his words had warmed her heart. What a nice thing to say. 'Well, thank you for the compliment.' Feeling self-conscious, she began fussing around with the bags of food, pulling containers out and setting them on the wooden table. 'Asian. Excellent. Do you want to eat with chopsticks?' She turned and began rummaging in a drawer in the sideboard.

'I think there are some disposable ones in the bag,' Richard said, after clearing his throat and giving his brain a bit of a jump-start.

'OK.' Feeling more and more like a deer caught in the headlights of an oncoming car, Bergan tried to think of what else she could do to keep her hands busy and her thoughts off the way Richard was making her feel. She closed the drawer and linked her hands together, hoping that by holding them it would stop them from trembling. 'What would you like to drink? I'm sorry, I don't have any wine. I probably should have thought to buy some for you as actually I don't drink alcohol.'

'At all?' He seemed surprised by that.

'No.'

'There's a reason behind that.'

'Of course there is,' she said, heading into the kitchen to collect a bottle of mineral water from the fridge. Once there, she closed her eyes and took three long and steadying breaths. It was imperative that she stopped behaving like an adolescent and started behaving like the intelligent woman she was. They were just eating food before going to the drop-in centre. That was all.

Feeling calmer, she returned with the bottle of drink and decided to lighten the mood presently surrounding them.

*'Monsieur?'* she asked, holding the bottle out to him as though she were a waiter asking the customer to check the vintage on a nice bottle of red.

*'Oui, mademoiselle. Très bien, merci.'*

With a smile she came round the table, opened the bottle and poured some into the glasses on the table. 'Even if I did drink, I would never drink any alcohol before heading to the drop-in centre. A lot of the kids who come there are battling addictions to alcohol, as well as other substances, and it's hardly fair for them to smell liquor on my breath while I'm talking to them.'

'Fair point.' He picked up his glass and held it out to her. 'A toast?'

Bergan acquiesced and picked up her own glass, waiting for him to speak.

'To being back on home soil—even if it is for a short time—and to making new friends.'

'New friends,' she repeated, and couldn't help but smile as she chinked her glass with his before both of them took a sip.

'Let's eat,' he said, and after sitting down they opened up the different containers, spooning the delicious food out onto their plates.

'How was your first lecture today? I'm sorry I wasn't able to make it, but I had a meeting with the hospital's CEO and I'd already changed it twice.'

Richard shrugged one shoulder. 'It went OK, I think.'

'Modest, eh? I heard there were people standing around the walls at the back of the lecture hall because there were no seats free.'

'I think everyone's more interested in checking out the new guy rather than what I have to say.'

'There's that modesty again. Do you enjoy lecturing?'

'I do, especially when what I'm relaying is new and exciting information on different techniques or advances in treatment plans.'

'It must be a little discombobulating—travelling all year long, fighting jet lag…' She smiled pointedly at him. 'Not to mention the language difficulties you must have faced.'

'You mean giving instructions in French?' He chuckled. 'Usually, I'm assigned a medical interpreter so that does make things much easier.' He swallowed his mouthful and took a sip of his drink before leaning his elbows on the table. 'OK. My turn to ask a question. Why don't you drink alcohol?'

Bergan had just put some food into her mouth when he asked the question and she simply stared at him as she slowly withdrew the chopsticks from her lips. She chewed slowly, as though considering his question, but she was really wondering just what she felt comfortable telling him. The truth? How would he handle that?

She finally swallowed her mouthful and took a sip from her glass. 'Guess,' she said, as she placed her chopsticks on the side of her plate and crossed her arms over her chest.

'A challenge. OK.' Richard nodded, pleased she hadn't shut him out. He quickly thought back over things she'd said since they'd met, pondering the way she'd been able to connect with Drak at the Moon Lantern festival and how she'd mentioned it wasn't fair for teens to smell alcohol on someone else's breath when they were battling an addiction.

'Teenage drunk?'

'Got it in one. I was a bad one, too.' She looked away from him and toyed with her chopsticks for a moment. Richard remained silent, watching the internal struggle taking place. Would she open up to him? Be honest with him? He'd told her the other day that he believed honesty to be the best policy, but whether or not she'd believed him was another matter. Now he hoped she did, hoped she'd take a chance and continue with what she'd been about to say.

Bergan consciously made herself stop fiddling with the chopsticks and calmly placed her hands in her lap and when she lifted her head, bravely meeting his gaze, her voice was clear and matter-of-fact.

'Three days after I turned fourteen I drank myself unconscious. I'd swiped a bottle of Scotch from my foster-father's liquor cabinet and had a party for one.'

Richard made a point of trying not to change his facial expression at this news. He'd seen first-hand, in many different A and E departments around the world, just how dangerous it could be for young teenagers to have that amount of alcohol in their systems. He listened intently as she continued.

'I drank myself unconscious.' She repeated the words slowly, a sad look in her eyes. 'I must have regained consciousness at some point and left the house. It's little wonder I didn't get hit by a passing car, but in the morning I woke up in some strange boy's bed, without a clue how I'd got there or what had happened.'

Richard swallowed, a bad feeling settling in the pit of his stomach. 'And the foster-father?'

Bergan pulled her loose hair back from her face, holding it suspended in her hands for a moment before allowing the glorious tresses to fall back into place. 'He gave me the beating I deserved for stealing his booze.'

Richard looked away from her then and shook his head. Not at what had happened to her in the past, but that her life had been that miserable that she'd ended up in such a dark place, at such a young and vulnerable age. What else had happened to her? Especially in such an environment? He could hazard a good guess and it wasn't at all pretty.

It also explained why she had a problem with dating and trusting men.

'I have a lot of baggage, Richard.' Again her words were matter-of-fact, as though she was trying to be strong and completely detached from her past. Why had he shaken his head? Had she completely turned him off? Wasn't that a good thing? She hadn't really wanted his interest in the first place so now that he knew the truth, he'd no doubt see the rest of the evening through and then their relationship could go back to being nice and professional.

'So I'm beginning to realise.'

Bergan clenched her jaw to stop the sudden pang of pain at his words. To think about scaring him off was one thing, but to actually hear him admit it was gut-wrenching. She knew it was better he left her life sooner rather than later, but deep down, in that small part of her that was still a scared little girl, she had hoped Richard might prove different from the other men she'd known, that he might be the man to help rescue her from the insecurities she'd buried so very deep.

She looked away from him, focusing on her glass, reaching out her hand to touch the inanimate object, focusing on its coolness rather than the fact that Richard might just get up and walk from the room without another word.

Richard put his own chopsticks down and leaned one elbow on the table, resting his chin on his hand as he looked at her. After his mother's words earlier he hadn't been at all sure what he might uncover about Bergan, but now all he could do was gaze at her with awe and admiration. He'd always liked to surround himself with people who were strong, who were able to overcome adversity.

Not only had Bergan managed that, but given her work at the drop-in centre, she was also willing to share her experiences, her thoughts and her emotions with teens who might find themselves in a similar position as she'd once been. That took a hefty amount of inner strength and a tonne of courage.

'And look at you now,' he continued, his rich tones washing over her. She raised her surprised gaze to his.

'What?'

'You're a successful doctor in a busy A and E department, but also spend a lot of your spare time reaching out to help kids who are in similar circumstances.' Richard leaned across the table and took her hand in his, holding it firmly as he continued to look her directly in the eyes, his blue gaze melding with her honey-brown one. 'You are quite an amazing woman, Bergan Moncrief, and I for one relish the challenge of getting to know you better. *Much* better.'

# CHAPTER FOUR

BERGAN WASN'T SURE exactly how she managed to keep control of the rioting emotions zipping through her body as she sat near Richard, staring into his hypnotic blue eyes. Where she'd thought he'd high-tail it out of her house as fast as possible, he'd completely surprised her by doing the opposite!

He was so different from every other man she'd met, and where, over the years, she'd thought that no man could ever surprise her again, Richard Allington was proving her wrong. Although she'd only known him a few days, he was definitely intriguing her, making her want to know more about him. The fact that she also found him incredibly handsome was both good and bad.

The way he looked at her, smiled at her, winked at her had the ability to set her body on fire. The fact that he could *do* that so easily brought with it a mountain of confusion and indecision. Should she even risk thinking about the possibility of something other than friendship existing between them in the future? Was that what he wanted or was she just someone to play with, a distraction to fill the hours when he wasn't at the hospital? Had he found a different woman in every country he'd visited?

There were just too many questions, too many unknowns, but even if she pushed them all aside, there was still one question she couldn't figure out—where had her self-control gone? She needed to figure out what it was about Richard that was wreaking such havoc inside her, and to do that she needed to be close to him, to spend time with him.

An experiment, a research project. That's what she needed to make it. She would treat this unwanted attraction towards him with all the same drive and attention she'd given to her medical research projects over the years. Doing research and conducting studies would help her to gain control over her senses and after that she'd be able to treat Richard like any other man of her acquaintance—with indifference.

She knew he would have plenty of flaws. All men did, and the sooner she discovered them, the sooner she could put him out of her mind and get on with her life. Four weeks. He was only here for four weeks and then he would disappear back to where he'd come from. It also meant, if she was determined to get to the bottom of this internal dilemma, that she would need to consciously spend more time with him…all in the name of research, of course.

Therefore, with clarity and logic starting to return, Bergan was able to finish her dinner, finding it was easier to gloss over what he'd said—that he was interested in getting to know her *much* better—and keep up a steady stream of conversation, mainly about the hospital and the drop-in centre. Thankfully, Richard had allowed her to chatter away, releasing her hand from his, leaving it tingling from his smooth, warm touch.

They'd been able to finish their meal and then get ready to head into the drop-in centre, but the moment they entered her car, Bergan once again became incredibly conscious of his closeness as he sat beside her in the passenger seat. *Keep it light, Bergan. It's just an experiment. Nothing more.*

Richard smoothed his hand over the soft leather seats and smiled. 'I had a car just like this, but in black.'

'When?'

'Before I left Paris.'

'You had a car in Paris? I didn't think that was the done thing. Everyone does a lot of walking in Paris, mainly because to drive in the traffic is bedlam.'

'So you *have* been there?'

'To Paris? *Oui, monsieur,*' she teased.

'I thought so. Generally, people can learn to speak French from a tutor, but to really speak French—proper French,' he added, 'it's best to stay in Paris for a while.'

Bergan drove along the darkened streets of Maroochydore, changing down gears as she neared a red light. When she'd stopped, she glanced over at him. 'Agreed.'

Richard's smile was small. 'So you stayed in Paris for a while? Worked there?'

*'Oui, monsieur,'* she repeated, a small smile playing on her lips, her tone deep, personal, intimate. He swallowed once, not missing the dip of her gaze as she took in the action, watching as his Adam's apple slid up and down his throat.

'I knew it. I knew you'd understood every word I'd said yesterday.'

Her smile increased and Richard once more felt as though she had just delivered a whammy of a punch directly to his solar plexus. She was incredibly alluring and he'd liked hearing her voice dip that extra half octave, as though she was speaking intimately to him, taking him into her confidence. It certainly didn't help that they were in such close proximity in the car. Her fresh, floral scent was enough to drive him to distraction and the fact that it was winding its way about him didn't help one bit.

Keep a clear head? When Bergan was around? It was

what he'd promised himself he would do, but now, sitting here, so close to her, he realised it was virtually impossible.

Richard couldn't believe the colour of her eyes. It was different, unique…it was Bergan. The colour of warm, rich honey and combined with her smile, her gorgeous pert little nose, her high cheekbones and smooth neck, it was clear why she'd been a regular feature of his dreams ever since he'd first seen her at the Moon Lantern festival.

And her hair… How his hands had itched to touch it, to run his fingers through the long, free, auburn locks. He'd watched, after they'd finished dinner, as she'd quickly and expertly plaited her hair and for some reason he'd been surprised at how intimate it had felt. It was as though he'd seen her put on a mask, keeping others at arm's length as she'd tossed the long plait carelessly down her back and straightened her shoulders. She'd put on her armour and was ready for action…and she'd allowed him to see it.

Now, as she sat next to him in the car, smiling that cute little smile of hers, he wondered what she'd do if he leaned over and brushed a sweet yet tantalising kiss across her lips.

He was a little surprised at the speed of his thoughts. Yes, he'd managed to go out on the occasional date over the past five years, but he certainly hadn't been captivated by any other woman as completely as he was with Bergan. Was that a good sign? To be moving this fast? It wasn't his usual style. Even with Chantelle things had progressed very slowly, but for some reason he simply couldn't stop thinking about Bergan and right now he couldn't stop thinking about kissing her.

Bergan's eyes widened a little and the smile started to slip from her lips as she stared into Richard's eyes. Was he thinking of kissing her? The question made her heart beat faster. What would she do if he did? Would she let him?

Would she slap him across the face? She didn't know and not knowing was the worst.

*Beep!* The sound of a car horn behind them, alerting Bergan to the fact that the traffic lights had changed colour, made them both snap out of whatever sensations had been pulsing between them and focus on getting to the drop-in centre without further incident.

As she drove, Richard tried to figure out exactly what it was about her that seemed to captivate him so much. He certainly wasn't the type of man to fall in and out of love easily—quite the contrary, especially as it was only five years since Chantelle had passed away. She'd told him to find someone else, that she would be sad to think of him spending the rest of his life living alone, mourning her. She had always been so bright, so cheerful, even during the last days when she'd been terribly weak from pain.

'Here we are,' said Bergan, turning into a driveway and parking next to a building that had certainly seen better days. It was clear people had been doing their best to spruce things up, with a large and colourful mural painted around the building.

'Who did the painting?' he asked as they climbed from the car. The wall was covered with a scene that showed people from diverse nationalities, of all ages and socio-economic situations living together in harmony.

'The kids did it, under the guidance of a seventeen-year-old boy called Drak. He's incredibly gifted when it comes to art.'

'Didn't he do the lantern for the festival?' Richard asked as they headed towards the front door.

'He did.' Bergan looked at him with a hint of surprise. 'How did you know that?'

Richard sheepishly shrugged one shoulder and shoved

his hands into his pockets. 'Uh…I sort of eavesdropped on your conversation with him at the festival. You wanted him to be proud of his lantern, to carry it with pride, and he didn't want to.'

Bergan nodded her head. 'He was a little vocal that night, but it wasn't because he was trying to be difficult. He's really quite a sensitive soul, but most of the time all people see are the piercings and tattoos.'

'Never judge a book by its cover.'

'An old cliché, but an apt one in this instance.' Bergan opened the heavy front door and Richard instantly helped her. 'Thanks. Come and I'll introduce you to the director, Stuart. He's amazing with the kids.'

She led the way to where a young man, dressed in dark jeans and dark T-shirt, a piercing or two in his ears and a 'sleeve' of tattoos on one arm, was leaning against a heavy wooden table, chatting with about five teens, discussing a new project the centre was trying to get up and running. If Bergan hadn't told Richard that Stuart was the director, he would have easily mistaken the guy for one of the teens who 'dropped in' here.

'They're all good ideas for how we can practically help the nursing home up the road.' Stuart glanced up and saw them walking towards him. 'And here's Bergan…and she's brought a friend with her.' Stuart instantly held out his hand to Richard as Bergan introduced them. Richard was conscious of the teenagers watching the adults interact and he received the distinct impression that all of them were putting up their barriers, no doubt an inbuilt habit when they met someone new.

'We're discussing the clean-up project at the nursing home,' Stuart explained to Richard. 'Trying to break down some stereotypes. Kids who dress in dark clothes, have a bit of ink and the odd piercing aren't necessarily bad or scary people. They're usually as lonely as half the residents of the nursing home.'

Stuart gestured to a few of the teens gathered around. 'Xenia suggested painting a mural at the front entrance as there's been quite a bit of graffiti on the nursing-home sign in the last month or two.'

'It wasn't us,' Xenia added hotly, draping her arm around the neck of the boy next to her and giving Richard a dirty look.

Richard nodded. 'Understood.'

'Aaron suggested helping with the gardening because, as you know, many of the able-bodied residents are keen gardeners, but aren't actually able to bend down or reach up high or even do too much manual labour, and this way they can also pass on their knowledge of gardening to the younger generation,' Stuart continued.

Aaron, a kid who was as skinny as a beanpole, had no ink or piercings and was dressed from head to toe in brown, nodded enthusiastically, his glasses, which were held together with a piece of sticky tape, almost falling off his nose. 'Old people like to talk and, well...Bergan's always saying we should listen more so...you know.' He shrugged.

A lot of the other kids agreed with Aaron and Richard was pleased to see that in here the breaking down of stereotypes had already begun.

'They're really good ideas,' Bergan agreed, nodding encouragingly at the gathered teens. She looked at Richard. 'What do you think? Any suggestions to add?'

Richard raised an eyebrow at the question then looked around at the group gathered before him. They really did look like a motley crew, but he knew from his work with teens of a similar age and circumstances that beneath all the ink and piercings they were just kids who were making the best of the bad hand they'd been dealt. The fact that they actually came *in* to the drop-in centre and were talking about actively participating in the community was huge.

'I think,' he said after a pause, 'these are excellent suggestions, and as the new guy I'll defer to the group. Although, whatever the final decision, I'd like to help.'

Before anyone else could say anything, a kid came bursting through the doors of the centre, his face red from running, an urgent and wild look in his eyes. Richard recognised him as the teen Bergan had been speaking to at the Moon Lantern festival—Drak. He was clearly out of breath and as he tried to speak, panting and puffing, Richard started to get a bad feeling in his gut.

'Jammo. Passed out. Bergan.' Drak gestured for her to come. 'Medical bag. Overdosed.'

'Not again.' Bergan was rushing towards a cupboard in Stuart's office. She quickly pulled out a set of keys from her pocket and unlocked the doors, taking out a portable medical kit that looked more like a toolbox and then quickly locking the cupboard again. 'This is the second time Jammo's tried something like this,' she muttered, clearly concerned.

'Whatever you ne—' he started to say, but she interrupted him.

'Come with me. Stuart, call the—'

'On it,' Stuart said.

Bergan nodded. 'Good. I'll call you when we have a location. Drak, lead the way.' The three of them raced out of the drop-in centre, running down the footpath, Bergan and Richard following behind Drak, who was sprinting ahead. He continued down the street, the three of them oblivious to their surroundings, the evening traffic starting to pick up in numbers. Car horns honked, engines revved and music blared from stereo speakers.

Bergan was only conscious of following Drak's lead,

sensing rather than seeing that Richard was still beside her, his strides slightly longer, which meant he was keeping pace with her, ensuring she wasn't left behind. He also reached down while they were running and took the medical kit from her hand.

'I've got it,' he said, barely seeming out of breath.

'Thanks,' she answered as she noted that Drak had turned the corner. They followed him into an older-style, multi-storey apartment block, one that had certainly seen better days, with a few of the windows boarded up thanks to a few smashed windows here and there.

'She's in here,' Drak panted, as he began taking the stairs two at a time. 'She's in Smitty's old place,' he continued, his eyes still reflecting his fear for the worst.

As Bergan rounded a landing on the stairs, she caught Richard's glance and saw that he looked in control and reflective, as though he was trying to go through a thousand different scenarios, wondering exactly what they might find when they finally reached Jammo. Bergan knew because she was doing exactly the same thing. She quickly pulled out her cell phone and passed the location information on to Stuart, who informed her the ambulance was on its way.

'Drak,' she called, as he started up another flight of stairs.

'Not much further,' he stated, but kept going.

'Do you know what Jammo took? Was it pills? An injection? Any clues?' Bergan held on to the handrail to ensure she didn't miss her footing on the steps, grateful Richard had thoughtfully taken charge of lugging the medical kit.

'There were pills next to her. I…I was going to bring the bottle with me, but I was just so scared that I forgot and ran to get you,' he panted, still going up the staircase. Thankfully, when they came to the next landing, Drak flung open the door and headed into the corridor.

Within another half a minute they were inside Smitty's old apartment, where Jammo was lying on the floor on an old mattress, seemingly lifeless. The young girl of sixteen wasn't moving, although, as they'd rushed into the room, Bergan thought she'd detected the slight rise and fall of the girl's chest.

Richard instantly dropped to his knees, opened the medical kit and pulled out two pairs of gloves, handing one pair to Bergan. She pulled them on and reached for the bottle Drak was holding out to her. Richard called to Jammo but the girl didn't respond. They shifted her onto her side in case she vomited. They didn't want her to choke. He reached for the penlight and checked her pupils.

'Sluggish but reacting to light.'

'Pulse is slow and weak.'

'What did she take?' Richard asked as he reached for the stethoscope.

'Temazepam. I don't know how many, but the bottle is empty.' As Bergan and Richard continued to treat Jammo, Richard motioned to the girl's wrists, which were both bandaged.

'How long ago did she do that?'

'Two weeks. She ran away from the hospital the day after she was admitted. I managed to check on her a few times and she seemed to be doing OK. Jammo? Can you hear me?' Bergan called, raising her voice. 'Come on. Come round.'

'Cardio is weak. She needs oxygen.'

'She's going to be OK, isn't she?' Drak asked, and Bergan glanced up at the small thread of fear in the words. It wasn't like Drak to show such an intimate emotion and Bergan couldn't help but wonder if there wasn't a deeper connection than she'd thought between the two teens.

'I don't know,' she answered him truthfully. 'You did

well to come and get us, but her body's already weak from losing a lot of blood the other week.'

'She's depressed,' Drak offered, by way of explanation.

'I'm not interested in the whys and wherefores at the moment, Drak,' Bergan reassured him calmly, as she took the stethoscope from Richard and listened to Jammo's heartbeat for herself.

'Skin is cold and clammy, lips are blue, fingernails are pale.'

'Prep for possible cardiac arrest,' Bergan said, and he nodded, looking into the medical kit for whatever he might need in case Jammo's heart stopped. 'Drak, why don't you go down and meet the ambulance? Let them know I'm here and get them to bring oxygen on their first trip up those stairs.'

'I don't want to leave her,' Drak said, which only confirmed Bergan's suspicions.

'You can help Jammo by getting those paramedics up here with the oxygen, ASAP. Here...' Bergan held out her cell phone to Drak. 'Take this with you. Richard's number is programmed in, so call him if you need to speak to either one of us.'

Drak hesitated for a moment.

'I promise to take good care of her,' Bergan told him, earnest sincerity in her tone. 'Didn't I take good care of her last time?'

'Yes.'

'Then trust me, Drak. You know you can.' She waved the phone in his direction and after hesitating for a moment longer he took the device from her and headed out of the room. 'Jammo?' Bergan called. 'Can you hear me? Come on. Come round. Do it for Drak.'

'Repeat obs,' Richard stated, and she agreed. Until they had Jammo back at the hospital, where they could at least perform a gastric lavage, all they could do was monitor her and try to make sure she didn't go into cardiac arrest.

No sooner had they started the next set of obs than Bergan shook her head. 'She's slipping.'

Richard listened to Jammo's heartbeat. 'Agreed.'

Bergan pressed her fingers to Jammo's pulse. 'It's stopped,' she said, and Richard nodded in agreement.

Together, they rolled Jammo onto her back before Richard placed a special expired air resuscitation mouth shield over Jammo's mouth and nose. Bergan readied herself to perform cardio-pulmonary resuscitation. Working together as a well-oiled team, they counted out the breaths and beats, determined to get the young teenager's heart started again.

While Richard breathed a few more breaths into Jammo's mouth, Bergan checked the girl's pulse. 'It's there. Just.'

He exhaled heavily with relief. 'Good.' He glanced across at Bergan, who was also smiling, pleased with what they'd just managed to do. 'She's by no means out of the woods,' he continued.

'But at least she's breathing.'

'Let's get her into the coma position while we wait for the paramedics to make their way up all those stairs. Why couldn't Smitty live on the ground floor?'

'Smitty doesn't live here anymore.'

'So where did he move to?' Richard asked, as they made sure Jammo was as comfortable as possible, Bergan hooking the stethoscope into her ears in order to check Jammo's heart again.

She listened intently then removed the stethoscope before looking at Richard. 'He died. Overdose in this very room.'

'Poor kid.'

'Smitty wasn't a kid. He was a druggy that a lot of the

foster and street kids came to when the foster-parents beat them or didn't feed them, or life just got too tough. They needed a place to crash. Smitty's—this place, for all its filth—was a safe haven for so many kids. He always offered whatever he had—food, drink and a piece of floor for them to crash on.

'He wasn't a dealer or a pimp and when he wasn't as high as a kite he did a lot of good things for a lot of the kids. He'd tell them they were stupid to take drugs, but then he'd go and shoot up, saying it was too late for him.'

There was a sad, melancholy tone to her words and Richard watched her with increasing confusion. Even though he'd only known Bergan for a few days, he knew her well enough to realise she didn't open up to everyone like this. She kept her hands busy, feeling Jammo's pulse, and not once while she was talking did she make eye contact with him.

'Drugs were Smitty's mistress,' she continued after a moment. 'He told me that once and there was a deep sadness and regret in his eyes. As though he wanted, so much, to go back and live his life again, but knew that was impossible.'

'You sound as though you admired him.' Richard kept his tone quiet as he checked Jammo's eyes.

'I did, in a way.'

'How old was he?'

'He would have been fifty-nine next month, if he'd lived.'

'Wow. I hadn't expected him to be *that* old.' Richard found it difficult to keep the surprise from his voice. 'You sound as though you knew him quite well.'

'Yes. Yes, I did.' It was only then that Bergan raised her gaze, slowly, to meld with his. 'Smitty was my father.'

# CHAPTER FIVE

DRAK WAS QUICK in bringing the paramedics up to Jammo and when they arrived Richard and Bergan worked with them to insert an intravenous drip into Jammo's foot, as she'd attempted to slash her wrists only weeks ago. With an oxygen mask over her mouth and nose, the teenage girl's observations began to stabilise.

'I'm going with her,' Drak declared protectively.

'Absolutely.' Bergan placed a reassuring hand on his shoulder.

'They can't make me leave her side when we arrive at the hospital, can they?' His eyes were scared, wild, determined. The last thing either Jammo or Drak needed now was a scene in the A and E department.

Bergan shook her head. 'Tell whoever you see at the hospital that you know me and that I say it's fine for you stay with her—as long as you don't interfere with the treatment. Stay in the room, out of the way, and I'll be along shortly.'

'Thanks, Bergan.' Drak, looking paler than she'd ever seen him, surprised her further by pulling her close for a hug. Tears instantly sprang to her eyes and a lump formed in her throat at the action, and although it was over almost before it had begun, she knew in that one moment that Drak had changed from a troubled teenager into a man with direction. Before she could say a word, he climbed into the back of the ambulance and Richard shut the doors, tapping twice to let the driver know he was clear to leave.

Bergan sniffed and swallowed, blinking away any sign of the emotional tears before she looked at Richard. He was standing beside her, the medical kit from the drop-in centre beside him on the footpath. 'Shall we head back?' she asked, indicating the way back towards the centre.

'Good idea.'

There was no hurry now, and as they walked along, Richard carrying the medical kit, Bergan began to feel highly self-conscious at having revealed so much about her past. The sun had set, the stars were starting to twinkle in the sky, the streetlights had come on and a warm breeze floated around them, almost like some sort of cocoon, keeping them separate from the world.

'Interesting, isn't it?' Richard said after a moment.

'What is?' She almost jumped at the sound of his voice and looked across at him, her defences up in case he said anything personal.

'Watching a boy turn into a man.'

'Oh. Drak. Yes. Yes, it is.' She nodded as they walked along. Her arms were crossed over her chest as though she was giving him a silent signal not to venture into personal matters. 'I can't deny that it makes me feel good. I've known him for quite a few years and it most definitely hasn't been smooth sailing.'

Richard chuckled. 'I can well believe it, but tonight… tonight I think the message you've been trying to get through to him, whatever it might have been, has finally hit its mark.'

'He *hugged* me. Voluntarily!' Bergan couldn't keep the delight from her voice or the smile from her face. 'It's moments like that that make everything I do, everything I try to teach these kids, worth it.' The smile slowly slid from her face and Richard couldn't help but watch her as they walked out of the glow of one of the streetlights and headed into the comfortable darkness. 'I'm just sorry his realisation came out of Jammo's terrible situation.'

'She has a good chance of recovery, and who knows? Perhaps Drak can get through to her.'

'Hope. There always has to be hope.' Bergan walked past the next lamppost, skirting around the outside of the glow it emitted, but Richard paused, staring at her.

'What did you say?'

Bergan stopped walking and turned to face him, dropping her arms back to her sides. 'Why?' Was that astonishment she heard in his tone?

'Just...please? Repeat what you said.'

Confusion marred her brow. 'There always has to be hope?'

He frowned then gave his head a shake. 'Perhaps it was the tone you said it in.' He closed his eyes and exhaled slowly. 'Never mind.' He started to walk again, stepping out of the light.

'You're confusing me. What did I say that was wrong?' Bergan fell into step beside him.

'Nothing. You said nothing wrong. I...knew someone who used to say that all the time. For a second there you sounded *exactly* like her.'

*Her?* Bergan's curiosity was definitely piqued. Someone from his past? Someone who was important to him? A girlfriend? An ex-lover? She pushed the thoughts from her mind. If Richard wanted her to know, he'd tell her. She'd learned of old that no good ever came from prying and pushing people when they didn't want to open up. Still, it made him far more intriguing.

They walked in silence for a while then Richard said,

'You're not going to ask me anything? Try and find out more about this woman I mentioned?'

Bergan glanced at him. 'Do you want me to?'

Richard passed another streetlight and Bergan could clearly see the smile tugging at his lips. 'Psych one-oh-one, eh? Answering a question with another question?'

Bergan couldn't help but return his smile. 'Well, you either want to talk about her or you don't. If you do, I'll gladly listen. If not, I'll respect your privacy.' She glanced down at the ground before crossing her arms once more over her chest. 'And…I'd like to thank you for respecting my privacy earlier and not trying to get me to open up more about… well…about what I said about my…father.'

'Hippocratic oath.'

'I'm not your patient.'

'OK. How about the friendship oath?'

'Friendship?'

'Is this not a friendship date? Are we not becoming friends?'

'I guess. Especially as I don't usually blurt out my past to just anyone. In fact, only Mackenzie knows the full truth about my upbringing, mainly because she was a part of it.'

'And your other friends?'

'Reggie and Sunainah,' she supplied, then shrugged. 'They know bits, as do your parents, but they're all more than happy to just accept me for who I am today. It's nice. Refreshing. Rare.'

'Those types of people definitely make the best friends.' Both were silent for a moment before Richard said, 'It hasn't been easy, this past year, on the fellowship, to make many new friends.'

'Four weeks here, four weeks there. Different countries, different languages, different traditions.' Bergan nodded. 'I can see that.'

'Hence the recent idea of the friendship date. And I have to say I'm really glad you agreed to let me into your world tonight, Bergan.' They weren't far from the drop-in centre and after they passed another streetlight and entered darkness again, Richard stopped, glad when Bergan followed suit.

'I don't have that many close friendships. A lot of men don't,' he said by way of explanation so she didn't think there was anything wrong with him. 'I have colleagues spread around the world and I'd classify a lot of them as friends, but *real* friends—people I can rely on at any time, any place, anywhere—are few and far between.'

Bergan nodded, her eyes adjusting to the darkness around them so she could see the lines of confusion creasing his brow and hear the hesitation in his words. He shifted the medical kit to his other hand, removing it as a barrier between them.

'I haven't known you long, Bergan, and yet I feel a connection to you. I think it's important you know that.'

'I sort of guessed when you asked me out.'

He smiled. 'Well, I can't deny that I find you attractive, but that's not entirely what I meant.'

His words warmed her through and through. She wished he wouldn't talk like that, so openly, about this strange attraction that seemed to exist between them, because it made her feel all uncertain and soft and feminine. She wasn't used to feeling this way and the intensity of her feelings was starting to cloud her thoughts. 'I… It's just…from my point of view, it would be far easier for me to deal with if you *only* found me attractive, on a superficial level, I mean, not…' She stopped and sighed, not sure what she was trying to say.

'Not connected on an intellectual and emotional level as well?' he finished for her.

'Exactly.'

'I can't say I understand what this…thing…is between us, Bergan—'

'Me neither.'

'But it's there and that in itself is a surprise and it's rare.'

'Yes.' The word was a whisper and as he continued to look down into her eyes, he saw a small smile touch her lips. It was the sign he needed, to know that whatever existed between them they were both on the same page. He breathed out slowly, enjoying this moment for what it was.

He stared at her, and she stared at him, yet there was no discomfort. 'Hope,' he said softly. 'There always has to be hope.' Richard spoke slowly, each word enunciated with deep emotion. 'Those were the last words my wife ever spoke to me.'

'Dr Allington?' One of the ward sisters seemed astonished to find him waiting in the nurses' station, especially at almost five o'clock in the morning. He was unsure whether he needed to ask for permission to see a patient.

'At least you know who I am,' Richard stated, smiling at her.

'I…er…was at your lecture yesterday. It was great to learn about the new techniques and equipment being used in emergency medicine.'

'Thank you…' Richard looked at the woman's name badge '…Ayana. It's very nice of you to say so.'

'Oh.' Ayana returned his smile. 'You're welcome. Er… so…um…' She appeared a little flustered in his presence and Richard wondered if he shouldn't have called ahead first. 'What can I help you with?'

'Nothing too bothersome. I only wanted to check on Jammo. We accident and emergency doctors don't usually spend a lot of time on the wards so I wasn't sure of the protocol and decided to just to wander up.'

Ayana reached for Jammo's case notes and handed them to him so he could read the charts for himself. 'She's doing much better. The last time she was in here, which I think was about two weeks ago, she discharged herself within twenty-four hours. At least this time she's stayed a little longer. We might actually be able to do something to help her.'

Richard perused the notes. 'Just over forty-eight hours since we brought her in. It's good to see she's recovering well, and I see she's even seen the social worker?'

Ayana nodded. 'Let's hope we get can through to the poor girl this time.' The sister shook her head. 'Only sixteen. She has her whole life ahead of her.'

Richard nodded and handed the notes back to Ayana. 'Yes. Yes, she does. Is it all right if I just look in on her? I won't wake her up if she's sleeping.'

'That's fine. That bed over there, with the curtain around it. She's very self-conscious and having the curtain drawn seems to help her.'

'Thank you, Ayana.' Richard smiled politely then walked quietly across towards Jammo's bed. Jaime Purcell was the girl's real name, but it stated clearly in her notes that she was to be called Jammo as her first name upset her. Richard could only imagine what the young girl had been through, but all of that was in the past and there was definitely hope, just as Chantelle had always told him. Hope. There always had to be hope.

He slipped carefully and slowly behind the curtain, not wanting to startle the girl if she was indeed awake. Thankfully, he found her sleeping. He wasn't surprised to see Drak sitting in the chair, which had been pulled close by the bed, the two teenagers holding hands. Drak was also sound asleep, resting his head against the edge of the mattress.

'They make a cute couple.'

It was only then that Richard looked over to the other side of the bed, in the shadows near the blind-covered window, and realised that Bergan was standing there.

'I didn't see you,' he whispered, and stepped over to where she stood so their voices didn't carry.

'Drak has barely left her side since she was admitted.'

'Is he also the reason she hasn't tried to discharge herself?'

'He is.' Bergan sighed. 'He's such a good man. He knows Jammo's been through the wringer.' She glanced up at Richard. 'Have you read her file?'

He nodded. 'I had a quick glance.' He also knew exactly what Bergan *wasn't* saying. Back in the earlier section of Jammo's case notes there were several admissions to A and E noted, beginning way back when the girl had been only two or three years old. Admissions for excessive bruising, burns and broken bones. Later, when the girl had been fourteen, she'd been admitted for treatment following a botched abortion attempt.

'Drak won't push her, won't rush her. You were right the other night when you said he grew up right before our eyes.'

Richard thought back to that night when, after he'd admitted to Bergan that he'd previously been married, they'd made their way back to the drop-in centre and after giving Stuart and the rest of the young people there an update on the situation, Bergan had driven them to Sunshine General's A and E department, where they'd been pleased with the way Jammo had responded to treatment.

Afterwards, Bergan had driven them home and, after thanking him for his help and for the dinner, she'd headed into her house, leaving him wondering if perhaps he shouldn't have said anything about Chantelle at all. Bergan certainly hadn't wanted to talk about it, to ask him questions, like any other woman would have, and that's when it had finally twigged that she *really* wasn't like other women.

She had a calmness about her, a peace that said she accepted people for who they were now, rather than who they might have been before. It was a little odd, but very refreshing and, given the little snippets she'd let slip about her own childhood, it was no wonder she was more than willing to give people a second, third, even fourth chance and probably more.

This revelation only succeeded in making him like her even more and for the next few days after their so-called 'date' Bergan had kept her distance from him. Whether or not she'd been excessively busy or avoiding him, he had no idea. While she might accept people for who they were, he'd also realised it was more than likely that she didn't like being at odds with herself. The fact that both of them could feel and admit there was something…different existing between them was something neither of them had expected.

'Everything still calm in A and E?' she asked a moment later, but before he could answer, Drak shifted and lifted his head. He checked Jammo was all right, placed a soft kiss on the girl's hand then repositioned his head and closed his eyes again.

'Perhaps we should go somewhere else to talk,' he suggested, and she instantly nodded, slipping out through the curtain and holding it open for Richard to do the same.

'Cafeteria?' she asked.

'Sure. I could do with a cup of tea, especially after the night we've just had.'

'I hate multiple motor vehicle accidents,' she said, after they'd stopped and said a brief goodnight to Ayana. 'But I love working in Emergency. I love being there to make a difference, to save a life, to give the patient the best possible chance of recovery.'

'Every day is different,' Richard agreed. 'While I think we all like the quiet days simply from the perspective that no one needs our help, they can make a well-oiled A and E team go stir crazy.' They headed out into the quiet and deserted corridor. 'I've seen it in every hospital I've worked in.'

'Really?'

He nodded. 'There are many cultural differences, but that's the one fact that stays the same. The opposite, of course, is true, that when the emergency room is hectic, that same well-oiled team takes pride in doing everything they can to save a life...and if they're not successful, the next few minutes are the same the world over.

'That moment when everyone pauses, unable to believe they weren't successful. The clock ticks on, the second hand so loud and unnerving, and although you know it's moving, somehow the world seems to stand still. Then someone calls the time of death and everyone's jolted back into action, following the necessary protocols and doing what needs to be done, knowing there will always be the opportunity to grieve at a later stage.'

'It's so true.' She gave him a grim smile. 'Although I don't recall seeing a talk entitled "A global look at intra-professional behaviour during intense medical procedures in the accident and emergency department" on your lecture schedule.'

He grinned. 'No, but now that you've given me such a great title, perhaps it's worth pursuing.'

'Make sure you give me a credit.' She laughed as they entered the cafeteria. Like the corridors, it was mostly deserted, the catering staff having long gone home and the vending machines scattered around the hospital fulfilling their purpose. The hospital, however, did supply staff with free tea and coffee, and Bergan and Richard made a beeline for the urn.

'All you did was give me a title,' he stated, spreading his arms wide, a broad smile on his lips.

'And without it you'd have no paper.' She shrugged as though that ended the debate. They made themselves tea and sat down in the chairs, grateful to finally be off their feet. Bergan slouched forward onto the table, needed its support for her exhausted body. 'It's not until I sit down that I realise how tired I am, but the instant I do, it hits me like a tonne of bricks.'

'I know what you mean.' Richard sipped his tea. They both remained silent for a few minutes, and he was surprised at how comfortable it felt. The other night, after he'd mentioned his wife, their companionable silence had changed into an awkward one.

Thinking about that now caused him to frown. Why *didn't* Bergan want to know about his past? Did she really just see him as someone who was passing through, only in her life for a short period of time so there was no real point in getting to know him any better? It also wasn't like him to be ready to reopen old wounds, to talk about his grief, to open up that one part of his life that he usually kept completely hidden from everyone.

The subject of Chantelle was special, precious and his. A part of him appreciated her not pressuring him to open up; the other part, the one that was now rearing its ugly head, was quite the opposite and for the first time in a long time he realised he *wanted* to talk about his wife, to share her life with someone new.

'Why are you frowning?' Bergan asked, and it was only when she spoke that he realised she'd moved. She was now leaning her arm on the table, her elbow bent, her head propped up on her hand as she held the cup of tea with her other hand and took a sip of the hot liquid.

Richard looked at her for a moment before raising a hand to his forehead, feeling the deep grooves there. 'Am I?' He instantly tried to relax his facial expression, especially as it appeared to be under such close scrutiny. 'Sorry. Didn't realise.'

'Worried about some of the patients we saw tonight? Although A and E is far quieter than it was just a few hours ago, I do feel sorry for the theatre staff because a lot of them still have quite a few more hours of work to get through before they can come and slump into a chair and drink a mediocre cup of tea.'

Richard's smile was instant. 'You're so right.'

'So,' she said, taking another sip of her tea, 'why were you frowning? Although,' she continued, as quickly as she'd first spoken, 'if you'd rather not tell me, that's fine. I'll respect that, but I will let you know that I'm also quite a good listener.'

He pondered her words for a moment before nodding. 'Fair enough. Well, Dr Freud, I actually do have a question for you.'

'For me?' Bergan eased up from her slouched position, flicking her long auburn plait back over her shoulder.

'Yes.' Richard paused, wondering how to broach the subject delicately, not wanting to put her on the spot but also trying to figure out why she wasn't that curious about his past. He had to admit he was more than a little curious about hers, and while he respected her privacy, he did hope that soon she'd be able to trust him with more. It wasn't that he wanted to gossip, it was simply because…he liked her.

'So what's the question? Do I have to guess?'

He smiled and shook his head. 'No. I was just trying to find the right way to phrase my words.'

Bergan sipped her drink again, watching him closely and making him feel highly self-conscious.

'Well…to answer your question, I was thinking about the other night, with Jammo and what happened after we'd put her in the ambulance.'

'OK.'

'I guess I've been wondering ever since we had our little…chat, on the way back to the drop-in centre, whether or not you were…' He stopped and shook his head. 'I'm afraid this will, no doubt, sound horribly vain, but here goes.' He straightened in his chair before holding her gaze. 'I've been wondering whether or not you're interested in me, in my life. I mentioned my wife and you barely batted an eyelid. Any ordinary woman would have plied me with questions—'

'Indicating you already know what the answers are going to be,' she returned, her tone quite calm and controlled.

'Sorry?'

'If other women have asked you about your wife, then you no doubt have your answers perfectly rehearsed.'

Richard scratched his head. 'I'd never thought of it like that before.'

'And if I were to ask you about her now, would your answers be the same ones you've given to other interested women?'

'Uh… I… Actually, I don't know. You've really thrown me for a loop, Bergan.' He pushed both hands through his hair, leaving it sticking out a little and making him look even cuter. Bergan tried not to smile. 'You do that, you know. From the way you look at me across a crowd of thousands or whether we're sitting quietly in an almost deserted cafeteria at…' He stopped and checked his watch. 'Almost a quarter past five in the morning.'

'And you're not used to such attentions from a woman?'

'That's a loaded question.'

'Is it? Have you dated much since your wife passed away?'

'How do you know she died?' he asked. 'I might have been divorced.'

Bergan instantly shook her head. 'Not with the way you spoke about her the other night. The loss, the grief, the resigned acceptance to continue living your life—it was all there in your tone and body language. And as to why I didn't ask you more about her, I was merely giving you room, as you've clearly been giving me room.'

'What do you mean?'

Bergan looked down at the half empty cup of tepid liquid in front of her. 'I blurted out something about my past, my personal life to you. You know about Smitty and yet you didn't push for all the sordid details.'

'I respect your privacy.'

'As I do yours.'

Richard leaned back in his chair and crossed his legs out in front of him. 'We're both too polite for our own good, is that what you're saying?'

'Got it in one.' She smiled at him.

'I'm curious about you.'

'Ditto.'

'Really?'

Bergan winked at him, feeling a little bolder than usual. Richard was interested in her. She didn't think she was anything special and yet he'd not only admitted to finding her attractive, but he really was interested in *her*. 'I'll share, if you will.'

'Just like that? You'll trust me?'

She shrugged one shoulder. 'You've proved yourself worthy.'

'How did I do that?'

'By checking on Jammo. It shows you really care.' Bergan held his gaze. 'I like that in a person.'

'Oh. So you *do* like me?'

She nodded, slowly and steadily, her expressive honey-brown eyes speaking volumes. 'Far more than I'm comfortable with.'

# CHAPTER SIX

RICHARD LOOKED AROUND the cafeteria, noticing the other group of people was getting up to leave. Within another minute it was just the two of them in the large, silent room.

'Why does it bother you so much that you like me?' As he spoke, he edged his chair closer to hers, unable to be that far away from her, especially when she was admitting to their mutual attraction.

'Because I don't like being...tempted. It makes me feel out of control.'

Richard nodded. 'You've had to fight for that control. I understand that.'

'Do you?'

'I may not have had experiences similar to yours, but emotions of helplessness can come from all sorts of directions.'

Bergan nodded then asked the question that had been nestled in the back of her mind for the past two days. 'Will you tell me about your wife?'

Richard shifted in his chair and placed his hands onto the table, lacing his fingers together in a slow and very deliberate way. 'Her name was Chantelle. She was a French nurse and we worked together for many years, first in Australia, then in Paris.'

'Was she the one who told you about the job there?'

He nodded. 'Yes. We were very good friends and then slowly that friendship evolved into more, into love.'

Richard looked down at his hands, his fingers clenched tightly together. 'Then, at the ripe old age of thirty-one, Chantelle was diagnosed with breast cancer.'

Bergan shook her head. 'Oh, Richard. So young.'

'She fought for her life, did everything the doctors prescribed—surgery, chemotherapy—but it was too late. The cancer was…ferocious.' A sad smile came to his face. 'I remember the day we went shopping for her first wig. The French most certainly know the art of wig-making and we found her a beauty. A glorious red and gold, much the same colour as your hair. Beautiful it was, and Chantelle looked very fine in it. She said she didn't want pity, she didn't want sadness, she wanted to enjoy every moment of life.'

When Richard's lower lip wobbled, just for a second, Bergan couldn't help herself and quickly reached out and placed a hand over his. Richard looked at her unseeingly as he looked into the past.

'I loved Chantelle, very much. But sometimes our life together seems more like a dream than a reality. A short dream filled to the brim with every emotion you could imagine. She had days of anger when she'd throw things in frustration. Other days, she'd ask me to hold her close and she'd just…weep. Her sobs were so gut-wrenching, so desperate, so honest.'

He closed his eyes and Bergan could see tears quivering on the ends of his eyelashes. She gave his hand a reassuring squeeze, wanting to let him know she was there for support. He'd been though his own grief, his own personal anguish and she had the sense that, like her, he didn't often talk about those deeper emotions.

Perhaps that was a part of why they'd been drawn together in the first place, the fact that both of them lived a life on the surface, quite happy and content up to a point, because deep down inside was a box of emotions that had been carefully locked away many years ago.

Bergan waited for Richard to collect his strength, simply sitting there quietly, holding his hand, wanting him to feel that she understood how difficult it could be to really open up that secret part of your life to someone else. It wasn't easy. It was often raw—the emotions rising up from the depths below, making a person feel exposed and vulnerable.

The last thing she wanted now was for Richard to feel uncomfortable, to feel as though he'd made a mistake in telling her about Chantelle, but when he finally opened his eyes and looked at her, she had the distinct impression that perhaps this was what he'd needed to do, to talk about his wife once more.

'She was so brave. She had bad days—the ones where she'd cry and rant and rave—but she only allowed herself to do that for twenty-four hours. The next day when she woke up she'd pick up her courage and strength and forge ahead once more.'

'Chantelle sounds like an amazing woman, Richard.' Bergan could clearly see him being married to a strong woman, and Chantelle certainly sounded like an incredible person.

'She was. The chemo, of course, used to take a lot of strength out of her, but she still managed to have a smile on her face, to have patience with those who nursed her.'

'Was she in a hospice?'

He shook his head, a small smile tugging at the side of his mouth. 'Did I mention how stubborn she was? She didn't want to take up a bed in a hospice when there were people worse off than her.'

'What did you do? I take it she stayed at home, then?'

'Yes.' The smile increased. 'When her mind was made

up, that was it. I cut back on my shifts and didn't work nights. Several of Chantelle's friends rallied around, rostering themselves to care for her whenever I was at work or to give me a bit of respite, a few hours when I could go to the shops and pick up groceries. Once, I thought about going to the movies, but it just didn't seem right to go without her.' He shrugged. 'That probably sounds silly.'

'No.' Bergan shook her head. 'Not at all. It can be difficult to try and find some enjoyment in the normal things we do when the person we usually did those normal things with is too sick to join in.'

'Yes. Yes, that's it exactly.' He exhaled slowly.

'How long were you married?'

'Fourteen months. She was diagnosed four months after our wedding.' He looked down at the way Bergan's hand was on his. Firm, understanding, supportive. He shifted his fingers, linking them loosely with hers before he spoke again, his tone dropping to a hushed whisper.

'She was so brave. She'd fought such a good fight. Then one day, with our close friends gathered around her bed, Chantelle looked at me, took my hand in hers and told me to move on with my life. She told me to find someone who'd give me a run for my money, who was stubborn, funny and kind. She urged me to find another true and honest love, filled with passion and power. I promised her, then I kissed her goodbye and it was then she told me never to give up hope.' A lone tear slid down Richard's cheek.

They sat in silence for a while before Bergan sighed and sniffed, unable to believe she was so affected by what Richard had shared. 'She chose how she would die. Not many people get to do that, as we know and see daily proof of.'

'True. I did envy her that. She planned her funeral, the food that would be served at her wake, the music I had to promise to play.'

'On a CD?'

'No. One song on the piano and the other on the guitar.'

'You play both instruments?'

He nodded. 'I do. I've actually found it very cathartic, playing music.'

'Will you play something for me some time?'

He was surprised at this, but instantly smiled and she was glad to see that happy, shining light back in his eyes. 'If you like.'

'Wow.' She wasn't sure why she was so surprised. Perhaps it was because learning a musical instrument was something she'd always wanted to do but had never really had the opportunity, so she admired anyone who could play. 'Are you any good?'

He chuckled. 'Too bad if I'm not. You've already asked me to play something for you so you're going to have to sit there and suffer through my bad renditions of jazz standards.'

'You must have had some talent if Chantelle wanted you to play at her funeral.'

Richard chuckled. 'You would think that. But let me tell you, while Chantelle was a very generous, very giving and kind person, she was also highly mischievous. I always thought she'd wanted me to play so that she could have the last laugh.'

Bergan giggled. 'She sounds like such a wonderful woman.'

'She was. I wish you two could have met.' Richard looked down at their hands, linked loosely together, before meeting her gaze. It had felt right to share with her and now it felt right simply to sit here and hold her hand. 'You're a lot like her, Bergan.'

It was such a very sweet thing for him to say, and combined with the way he was holding her hand and looking into her eyes, Bergan was astonished at the desperate longing winding its way through her, begging her to believe his words. She'd promised herself so many years ago that she would never believe the guff that men, in general, often spouted, but this time she really wanted to.

She swallowed, surprised to find her throat dry, and forced herself to look away from him. She needed to break the intense and intimate atmosphere surrounding them and racked her brain for something different, something mildly humorous to say. 'Apart from her wig,' she added, and was instantly rewarded with one of Richard's smiles.

No. She didn't want to think of it as a reward, she wanted to put distance between them because now that she knew about his past, now that he'd opened up to her and confided in her, he would no doubt expect the same from her.

It was all well and good to say that she trusted him, that she knew he would keep her confidence, but actually *talking* about her past was something she usually avoided at all costs. She looked at where their hands were joined, his thumb rubbing gently over her knuckles, causing little jolts of delight to travel up her arm before bursting forth and flooding her entire being.

'Yes. Before her hair came out, it was jet black, and for years I'd had to listen to her bemoan the fact that even though she'd tried to dye it red, it had never really worked. That's just the sort of person she was. Her hair fell out due to the extensive chemotherapy and she took that as a sign to go and buy a wig in whatever colour she wanted.'

'The glass is half-full, rather than half-empty.' Her words were softer than before.

'Exactly.'

Bergan shook her head. 'I'm not like that, Richard.' She glanced briefly at him as she tried to pull her hand away, but he held it firmly and looked into her eyes.

'I disagree.'

'You barely know me.'

'I know enough. I've seen the way you are with your staff in A and E, firm but fair. I've seen you with patients and with teenagers and with your friends.' He gave her hand a little squeeze, hoping to get his point across, hoping that she'd believe him. 'It doesn't matter to me what may or may not have happened in your past, Bergan, it's who you are *now* I'm interested in.'

She looked at him for one long moment before pulling her hand free and rising to her feet. She shook her head and began pacing up and down, never more pleased that the cafeteria was vacant.

'You shouldn't be.'

'Shouldn't I?' He couldn't help but give her a bemused smile.

'No.' She held out a stern finger towards him. 'Don't look at me like that with those big blue eyes of yours.'

'I didn't realise they caused so much damage.' He chuckled and shifted in his chair, about to stand and walk over to her. Bergan immediately stepped back and raised both hands.

'Don't be cute either.'

'Bergan…I'm—'

'Just stop. Please, Richard?' She took another step away and shook her head. 'I can't…think properly when you're near.'

'Isn't that a good thing?'

She glared at him before turning and pacing towards another table, pushing in a few chairs here and there, needing to do something so she could at least gather her thoughts. Finally, she looked across at him, pleased he was once more sitting down.

'There can never be anything between us. Not of a romantic nature,' she clarified.

'Why?'

The single, soft and totally reasonable question instantly exasperated her. She spread her arms wide. 'Because I'm damaged goods. I've done drugs, I was a teenage drunk. I've done some horrible things and half of them would make your hair turn white right here on the spot if you knew what they were.'

'I very much doubt that.' He stood, but she instantly pointed to the chair.

'Sit.'

With a small smile he did as he was bid.

'Thank you,' she said, trying to inject a little more control into her tone. Dragging in a deep breath, she slowly let it out before closing her eyes. Crossing her arms over her chest, needing to ensure her barriers were up when she spoke, she began.

'I didn't know Smitty was my father. Not for quite some time. Both my parents were druggies. I found my mother dead from an overdose, with the needle still in her arm, when I was only five years old. My father had left when I was a baby and with no other family to claim me, I was put into the foster system.' The words tumbled out of her mouth, clear and matter-of-fact, but Richard realised she needed to say them fast. She'd unlocked a door she'd slammed shut many years ago and now she wanted to deal with this and bolt it all back up as quickly as possible.

'Back then there weren't as many rules as there are now, no background security checks on foster-parents, just too many kids in an already-corrupt system. Thankfully things have improved, but, having been badly treated, I soon realised that the more havoc I created, the less the social workers interfered. I was branded a "difficult case" and left to fend for myself.'

Richard didn't want to interrupt, but when she finally opened her eyes and looked at him, he nodded, to indicate he was still listening. She seemed appeased by that and slowly, as she spoke, she began to pace back and forth.

'I did meet a few people whom I could trust. Poor Mackenzie was one of them. She was ten when we met and she was being picked on by the other kids in the foster-house she lived in. When I arrived, things changed.'

'You protected her.' He hadn't meant to speak, hadn't meant to break her concentration, but the words, filled with admiration and understanding, had left his lips before he could stop them.

Bergan stopped pacing and nodded. 'I was only a year older than her, but I started to realise that the two of us together were stronger against some of the older boys. If we stuck together, it meant protection for *both* of us and the next time the system tried to shift us, they rehomed us together.' Only now did she allow herself the brief glimmer of a smile.

'And Smitty?' Richard asked.

'I'm getting to that bit. Good heavens, you're impatient.'

He shrugged one shoulder but was pleased she wasn't pacing as much as before and had actually uncrossed her arms, shoving her hands into her trouser pockets.

'Like a lot of the other kids, at seventeen I tried my luck living on the street, but it's much harder than I'd thought—surprise, surprise,' she murmured with a hint of sarcasm. 'At any rate, I ended up at Smitty's place and I'd stayed there five nights before I even saw him.' She shook her head, gazing off into nothingness, remembering. 'He was actually quite lucid that first time and the instant he saw me he turned as white as a ghost. Before I could even introduce myself, he grabbed me by the shoulders and demanded I tell him my mother's name. I did, and then this weird man, with long hair and a shaggy beard, hugged me.

'"I'm your dad," he said. Then he told me exactly when my date of birth was, where I was born and how he'd insisted I be called Bergan, after some actress he'd had a crush on when he was a teenager. He also said I looked exactly like my mother and he'd initially thought she'd come back to haunt him.'

'What happened after that?'

'Nothing.' She spread her arms wide for an instant before letting them fall to her sides. 'I went to Smitty's, like every other kid, when I needed a place to crash or some food. I talked to him sometimes, when he wasn't either out of it or jonesing for a hit. There was food, not much but some. Blankets and some old mattresses. There was also running water, so if you could get someone to guard the bathroom door, you could actually have a shower.' She grinned. 'That was bliss. Anyway, in the end Mackenzie and I became regulars, stopping at Smitty's and helping to…er…collect more food.'

Richard's grin was wide as he understood her meaning of the word 'collect'.

'Then one day I came back and found Smitty stone-cold dead. It took me a while, but I finally remembered the name of a social worker who had helped him.' Bergan looked off into the distance. 'This woman was probably only about five or six years older than me, but the instant I looked into her eyes I saw genuine sorrow that Smitty had died. She called the ambulance, and before I left I asked her what would happen with the flat. Could we all still come here and not be hassled?'

'What did she say?' Richard was eager to know.

'She said she would look into ways of keeping it going.

More mattresses and blankets miraculously appeared, the cupboards were regularly stocked with non-perishable foods. It wasn't the best system in the world, but it was one that worked.'

'Do you still keep in contact with her?'

Bergan shook her head. 'One night she was admitted to A and E, motor vehicle accident. She was in a bad way and died twenty-four hours later.'

'But...Smitty's. It's still there and the kids still use it, right?' Richard frowned for a moment before he lifted his gaze to Bergan's. 'You pay the rent, don't you?'

She swallowed, knowing she shouldn't be surprised he'd figured it out. 'Mackenzie and I do it together. You've got to understand the importance of that decrepit little flat. The night Smitty died, I realised that if I didn't want to end up like my parents, I'd better make some changes. Just like Drak, I grew up in an instant. I used Smitty's address as a billing address and managed to get myself a part-time job as a waitress. After a month I had enough to share a small one-bedroom apartment with Mackenzie. I decided that instead of butting heads with the system, I had to learn to make it work for me. By the time I was eighteen I'd completed my higher school certificate and sat the entrance exam for medical school.'

'You're quite a woman, Bergan. But I knew that before you told your story.'

'Thank you, Richard, but the point of my *story* was to let you know that I'm bad news. I'm a train wreck.'

'I disagree.' He stood and shoved his hands into his pockets. 'I see a woman who, against the odds, has managed to not only make good but to help others along the way.'

'You're making it sound more important than it really is.'

'I don't think Mackenzie, or Drak or Jammo would see it that way. Bad things happened to you. I don't deny that, but look at what you've accomplished, Bergan. Look at how you relate to those kids at the drop-in centre.' He took a step towards her. 'How they look up to you. How you gave Drak strength not to be ashamed of his creative abilities.' He took another few steps before she stopped him.

'Stay right there.' She held up her hands. 'It feels like you're stalking me.'

Richard slowly shook his head. 'That wasn't my intention.'

'I can read in your face what your intentions are.'

'They're honourable, if that's what you're implying.'

'I'm not an honourable woman.'

'I beg to differ.' He took another step closer and came up against her upheld hands. The instant they made contact with his chest, the heat of her touch seemed to scorch him with delight. Bergan dropped her hands back to her sides, but before she could move back, Richard placed two gentle hands on her shoulders.

'You deserve a world of happiness, Bergan. Actually, you deserve more than that,' he said quickly. 'Two worlds. Two worlds filled to the brim with happiness and sunshine.'

Richard moved one hand to cup her cheek, tilting her head up a little, ensuring they were looking at each other as he spoke.

'I promise not to rush you. I promise to let you set the pace, but I won't let you push me away.'

'Richard?' she breathed, wanting to draw him near and push him away at the same time. There was confusion and apprehension in her eyes, and she was unsure what he might do or say next. She was still having difficulty believing he hadn't walked from the room in a fit of revulsion after what she'd told him. The last thing she'd ever expected had been for him to support her, to stand before her, telling her she deserved two worlds filled with happiness and sunshine! She gently shook her head from side to side. 'I don't—'

'Shh.' He placed two gentle fingers momentarily on her lips. 'Believe me, Bergan, when I say that I find you…exquisitely beautiful.'

'I can't.' The words were barely a whisper.

His smile was filled with understanding. 'They say it's easier to believe the bad stuff about ourselves than the good things. The fact of the matter is, though, that you *are* a beautiful woman, both inside and out. You care so much about others and you give and give and keep on giving.'

'But why do you…?' She stopped and closed her eyes, dragging in a breath before slowly letting it out. She looked up at him. 'I come with baggage.'

His smile was instant. 'We all do, but Chantelle showed me how to reach out and grab life with both hands, as well as remember that there's always hope. I thought I was doing that, especially when I agreed to the travelling fellowship, but I'm not sure I've been grabbing life at all.'

'So…' Bergan frowned. 'I'm not sure what you're saying, Richard.'

'I'm saying that I hope you'll allow me to see more of you, to spend time with you while I'm here in Australia.'

'More friendship dates?'

He shrugged. 'It's a good place to start, don't you think?' He stared at Bergan for a moment. 'Perhaps we've both thought we were grabbing life with both hands.'

'When really we weren't?'

'I get the feeling that you know what it's like to be truly lonely, Bergan. I know I do. Standing in a crowd, I can feel alone. By myself, I can feel alone, but that inner, dark loneliness…I think we tend to hide our true selves there.' He spread his arms wide. 'By talking to each other—by feeling *comfortable* to discuss those inner darknesses with each other—surely that's the first step on the road to the hope we both know exists but may not have felt for a very long time?'

Bergan pondered his words for a moment, trying to ignore the lump in her throat. What he'd said had been everything she'd been feeling, especially about the loneliness she'd carried around for most of her life. Surprisingly, she hadn't realised that Richard was also living in that dark, lonely place as well. Eventually, she sighed and lifted her gaze to meet his. 'We spend time together? Friendship dating?'

The slow smile that spread across his face managed to touch her heart as well as cause the butterflies in her stomach to take flight. She'd never been with a man who could make her feel pleasantly and excitedly unsettled with just a look, but Richard seemed to be an expert at it. 'Exclusive friendship dating,' he clarified.

'No—you know—hanky-panky?'

His smile broadened at her term. 'We'll take things as slowly as you like.'

'And when you leave? What then?'

He shrugged. 'Honestly? I don't know. When I leave Australia, I return to Paris where I have a two-week block of writing up and presenting my findings of the fellowship, and after that I'll be back to being just a regular doctor, working in a busy Parisian A and E department.'

'And you'll stay in Paris?'

Richard reached down and took both her hands in his. 'I don't know, Bergan. It's unusual for me *not* to know my next move because ever since Chantelle's death I've immersed myself in routine, in planning ahead, in hiding behind work. Perhaps it's time to make some changes.'

He raised her hands to his lips, pressing a soft kiss to her knuckles. Bergan gasped at the light contact, unable to believe the riotous way her body reacted to his delicate touch. 'All I'm certain of at this point, right now, is that I want to get to know you better.'

'Why?' The question was barely audible, but he heard it.

'Because you're an incredibly intelligent, beautiful and generous woman, Bergan. You're on my wavelength and...' He shook his head. 'I thought I'd *never* find that again. Yes, there are uncertainties, but perhaps, through forging a friendship, we'll be able to find some answers.'

'Help each other to step from the darkness into the light?'

'Yes.' He rubbed his thumbs over the tops of her knuckles, as though massaging in the small kiss.

'Friendship dating.' She spoke the words as though they were finally starting to make sense.

'Think of it like the old-fashioned way a gentleman used to court a lady. No pressure but lots of fun.'

'Court?'

'I said we'd take it slowly. Take it at your pace.'

Bergan angled her head, her eyes twinkling with a touch of repressed humour. 'What if my pace ends up being faster than yours?'

Richard's eyes widened with delight at her teasing words. They really *were* on the same wavelength. 'Then I'd ask you to respect my need to take it slowly.'

Bergan couldn't help but return his smile. Richard wanted to *court* her? As far as Bergan could recall, no man, not any she'd ever been remotely acquainted with, had ever *courted* her. She felt so incredibly out of her depth, but when she looked into Richard's blue eyes she found herself relaxing and sighing and wanting desperately to agree.

He was only here for another three and a half weeks, and it wasn't as though she could fall in love in such a short time. Besides, it would be nice to have some calm and controlled male attention for a change, and although she'd admitted to being attracted to Richard, she knew she was in no danger of falling in love. She didn't *do* love.

She concluded, therefore, that as Richard was allowing her to set the pace of this 'courting' thing, she really was in no danger whatsoever.

Slowly, she met and held his gaze, nodding her head in affirmation. 'OK, then,' she said eventually. 'You can… court me.' Even as she said the words she couldn't help but laugh and as Richard gathered her close, his warm, protective arms about her, she felt lighter than she ever had before.

Hope. She certainly hoped this was the right decision.

# CHAPTER SEVEN

'HOW LONG HAVE you been dating him now?' Reggie asked as she stirred her coffee.

'We're not dating, per se,' Bergan tried to protest, but even she knew that was exactly what she and Richard were doing, no matter what words they used to describe it.

'Then what would you call it?' Sunainah asked.

Bergan shrugged and sipped her coffee. 'We're...spending time together.'

'Dating,' Sunainah and Reggie said together. Bergan just shook her head and finished her drink.

'Richard calls it "courting",' she told her friends. 'It's cute and old-fashioned and quaint. I get his undivided attention without the stress of always thinking how to fend off groping hands. He's a perfect gentleman and I like it.'

'Break out the blue roses,' Reggie stated.

'Hey!' Bergan growled, frowning at her friend as the others laughed. 'I wish I'd never told you that.'

'What?' Reggie clutched her hands to her chest in a romantic gesture and sighed. 'I think it's a lovely idea, having blue roses at your wedding.'

'Blue roses are rare and hard to find,' Mackenzie added. 'The man who persists in breaking down all your barriers and loving you no matter what is the man who has figuratively searched for the blue rose and found one.'

Bergan shook her head. 'We were young, stupid kids when I said all that and besides…' she levelled a steely glare at her friends '…there's not going to be any wedding. We're just…you know, courting, and besides, he lives on the other side of the world.'

Bergan checked her watch and almost yelped at the time. 'I need to get back.' She jerked her thumb in the direction of Sunshine General Hospital, which was just across the road from the café she and her three friends tried to frequent whenever they could all meet up.

Four busy women with four busy schedules. Some weeks it was nigh on impossible and this week Bergan wouldn't have minded missing their catch-up as, although she loved her friends, she'd rather have spent the time with Richard. She also knew if she told her friends that, they'd read far more into it than was there.

'So do I,' Mackenzie said, and blew kisses to her friends as they stood from the table.

'Go on,' Bergan urged as the two of them walked back towards the hospital. 'Ask.'

'Ask what?'

'Oh, come off it, Kenz. You're dying to find out more information about Richard and me.'

'Am I? Well, OK, then. Has he kissed you yet?'

'No, and it's been two whole weeks since we started this courting thing.'

'Really? That long? That means… Wait a second. Richard leaves at the end of next week? That's gone fast.'

'It really has.'

'So you're…happy?'

'I am…but—'

'Uh-oh. There it is. What's wrong?'

'It's just…Richard has said I can set the pace, but I'm

still not sure *how* I'm supposed to do that. I've never been in this type of relationship before.'

'A healthy one?' Mackenzie couldn't resist teasing.

'Exactly. All my life I've been used to being put down by men, or abused in one way or another. Smitty was the first male who didn't seem to want anything from me.'

'Smitty didn't want anything from anyone—except his drug dealer.' Mackenzie's words weren't malicious, merely matter-of-fact.

'True.' Bergan sighed as they entered the hospital, the two women walking side by side, heading towards the A and E department. '*I'm* in a normal, healthy relationship. Who would have thought it?'

'Me.'

'Yes, but that's only because you're a newlywed and you think everyone should be as happy as you.'

'And aren't you?'

Bergan glared at her friend before swiping her pass card over the sensor to open the door leading to A and E. The first person she saw was Richard, standing at the nurses' station, chatting with one of the male registrars. Just at the sight of him her heart rate quickened, her palms seemed to perspire and her mouth went dry.

She stared at him, having not seen him since yesterday evening when he'd left her house after a quiet evening of a relaxing dinner followed by watching some television together. Again, that was something she'd never really done before—just sat and watched television in peace and harmony, Richard's arm around her shoulders, she leaning her head against his chest.

They'd laughed together, discussed different aspects of the show they had been watching and had generally had what most people would call 'a normal night in', but for Bergan it really had been like manna from heaven. When she was with Richard, she felt like a normal girl, in a normal relationship, with a normal boyfriend.

Even the word 'boyfriend' sounded strange when she thought about it, but she guessed that was the term her friends might apply. Before the evening had ended he'd arranged for her to go to his place for dinner where he would make good his threat to play something on the piano and guitar for her.

'Your mother has a piano? I don't remember seeing it.'

He'd nodded. 'In the spare room upstairs. Just a small upright, which I think might be a little out of tune. Must remember to call the tuner before they get back.' He'd made a mental note, but had held her hand firmly as they'd walked from her place to his.

'So...was that *you* playing the other night? I thought you had a CD on.'

'Oh?' He'd looked a little sheepish. 'I didn't think it was that loud. Sorry.'

'Don't be.' Bergan had shaken her head, smiling up at him in delighted surprise. 'I have a feeling that you definitely won't be assaulting my senses with your playing. That piece sounded incredible.'

'Er...thank you.'

'You're not used to people praising your musical ability?'

'I'm not used to *sharing* my musical ability. Playing an instrument is...personal. It's an expression of my inner feelings, my inner self, and as such I've rarely openly played for people, other than for my sisters and parents.'

'And Chantelle.'

'Of course.' They'd stopped outside his front screen door, just shy of the sensor light, and Richard exhaled slowly. 'There were several pieces, mainly Bach, that used to really soothe Chantelle into a nice, relaxed sleep.' His smile had increased. 'Then there were times when she demanded the "1812 Overture" because it gave her the strength to fight on.'

Bergan had sighed and slipped her arms around his waist, delighted that she had the right to do such a thing. 'You truly are a wonderful man, Richard. The more I learn about you, the more I like.'

'I'm going to take that as a huge compliment,' he'd said as he'd dipped his head and brushed a soft and tantalising kiss across her cheek. They'd stood there for a few more minutes, content to simply hold each other, before he'd kissed her cheek again and bidden her goodnight.

And that was the way it had been every time they'd parted at the end of the evening. He was always a perfect gentleman and sometimes she wished he wouldn't be. Was that wrong? After everything she'd been through? It wasn't that their dates weren't romantic because it was clear with the quiet intimacy they shared that Richard certainly took this courting thing very seriously.

Now, as he stood there, chatting with the registrar, his hair slightly messy where she knew he'd pushed his fingers through it, his stance casual but his shoulders back, indicating he was ready to spring into action the second an ambulance arrived, Bergan couldn't take her eyes off him, almost desperate for him to detect her presence.

Mackenzie was chatting away beside her, but Bergan wasn't listening, and when Richard finally turned his head and saw her standing there, that small, intimate smile that she was coming to recognise as being purely Richard touched his lips.

He was rostered on for the afternoon shift and it wasn't until now that she realised she'd been waiting through the long morning for this exact moment. Within a matter of seconds he'd excused himself from the registrar and was heading in her direction.

'Well,' Mackenzie said, sighing, 'I can see I'm superfluous here, so I'll just leave.' She waved to Richard as he came over.

'You're not leaving already, are you, Mackenzie? How was coffee with the girls?' He glanced once at Mackenzie and then at Bergan, where his eyes stayed, as though he needed to drink in every aspect of her. When Bergan didn't answer, Mackenzie chuckled.

'It was good. I've got to run. Clinic,' she said by way of explanation, and headed quickly towards the stairwell.

'So.' Richard crossed his arms over his chest and took a small step closer to her. Bergan couldn't believe the amount of pressure against her chest caused purely by his nearness. She could almost feel the heat radiating from his body, the way the spicy scent she now equated with him seemed to tease at her senses, the way she longed to have his big, strong arms wrapped around her. Why was it that whenever he was within touching distance she wanted to throw herself into his arms and to never let go? Was this a bad urge to have? Was this part of dating? Of what normal people, in normal relationships, did every day?

'I've heard that the morning has been rather quiet, emergency-wise.'

'Yes.'

'Do you want to give me a debrief? In your office perhaps?' he suggested, raising one seductive eyebrow. Bergan's eyes widened with excitement, which she quickly attempted to curb. She opened her mouth to reply, but no sound came out so she nodded instead. As she turned and headed down the side corridor towards her office, her heart rate beginning to increase due to his nearness, she heard Richard's warm, deep chuckle.

It was as though he could see quite clearly the way he affected her and she didn't mind one little bit. She simply couldn't help the thrill of delighted anticipation that pulsed through her at the thought that so very soon she'd be alone with Richard. How was it he could make her feel so pretty and feminine with just one look? His gaze had never been leering in any way, shape or form, but it left her in no doubt whatsoever that he was attracted to her.

As she withdrew her pass card from her pocket to pass it over the scanner, she was astonished to find her hand shaking slightly. That was odd. No man in her life had affected her in such a way. Usually she was able to read them like a book, knowing exactly what they wanted from her, and that way she could choose to provide it or reject the impulse.

She'd made a deal with herself to enjoy the time she had with Richard, to relax, which, for her, wasn't at all easy. Yes, he would be leaving at the end of next week, but she wasn't going to think about what happened next. For the first time in her life she was just going to go with the flow. It had been difficult at first, to really slip into the 'whatever' mode, but now she could definitely see the appeal. It felt as though she was on vacation…a vacation from her usual life. She knew it would end, that Richard would return to Paris and she'd get back to her normal daily routine, looking back on this time they'd spent together as nothing more than the equivalent of a shipboard romance.

The instant they were secure behind her closed door Bergan turned to face him and somehow found herself in his arms in a matter of seconds. She didn't try to pull away, but instead she held him as closely as he was holding her.

'Sorry if I startled you,' he murmured, the vibration from his words passing into her body, causing tingles to flood through her. 'I like it when you're close.'

'Don't apologise,' she whispered near his ear. 'I…like it, too.'

Richard edged back slightly. 'Really?'

'Why should you be so surprised? Can't you tell?'

His smile increased. 'Well, I knew you weren't averse to me holding you close, but I guess I'm pleasantly surprised that you've voiced it.' It meant he was definitely making progress. The fact that Bergan had come to mean a great deal to him in such a short space of time was something he hadn't wanted to fight. It also made him consider what might happen next. She hadn't said anything about his departure in ten days' time and neither had he, not wanting to spoil what they were enjoying right now. He brushed a soft and tender kiss across her cheek before gathering her close once more, breathing her in, closing his eyes and feeling the stress slip from his body.

'I don't understand it,' she said, her tone still a whisper as she wrapped her arms more securely around his neck, her fingers playing with the ends of his hair. He'd be due for a haircut soon, but right now she liked the way his short back-and-sides cut had grown a little, making it less severe.

'I don't know what it is about hugging you, holding you close, Richard,' she murmured softly, sighing into his embrace. 'But it strengthens me, it invigorates me, it lets me know that no matter what else happens in life, there is always somewhere I can feel safe. I've never felt that before and definitely not from just a hug.' She closed her eyes and breathed in his scent once more, relaxing against him, knowing his big, protective arms would never let her fall. 'I like it.'

'Me, too.' And he did. Being close to Bergan, actually having permission to hold her hand or put his arm around her or draw her near to him as he was now, had been an absolutely delight. Spending time with her had been a joy, especially their need to debate and discuss not only medical issues, but world events, too. She was his intellectual equal, as well as being highly compatible with him on the emotional side of things.

She'd become more open about her involvement with the drop-in centre and had listened to a lot of the ideas he'd put forward, the two of them moulding them into a more tangible format that she could then take to Stuart, the director.

Both of them had been delighted with Jammo's progress after her brief stay in hospital. Thanks to Drak, Jammo had agreed to talk to one of the drop-in centre's counsellors, as long as Drak went with her. Bergan had watched the two teens walking along, holding hands and smiling.

'We're taking it real slow,' Drak had told her after he and Jammo had finished the first counselling session. 'Jammo's been through heaps and I really like her. She scared me that night and now I wanna do right by her. So slow is best. You know, like in the olden days. Girls need to be made to feel special and stuff.'

Bergan had smiled. 'You both have plenty of time,' she'd confirmed, encouraging him to continue along this path. It wasn't until she'd arrived home that night to find an envelope taped to her front door, which contained an invitation to dine with Richard at his place, that she'd realised Richard's form of 'courting' was incredibly similar to how Drak was treating Jammo. The fact that she wasn't having to constantly second-guess Richard's motives, or fight off wandering hands, *was* making her feel 'special and stuff', as Drak had termed it.

As he held her now, she couldn't help pulling back a little and looking at him. 'Just out of curiosity, did you speak to Drak about how to take things slowly with Jammo?'

Richard raised an eyebrow at her question, blinking once or twice as though wondering where it had come from, but the cute smile on his lips gave away the answer. 'A few weeks ago. Sure. He wanted to know *how* to slow things down, but still let Jammo know he was interested. Sad that young men nowadays have no idea how to court.' He shook his head as he shifted his hands to her waist.

'I think it's nice.'

'That Drak's taking his time with Jammo or the ethics of courting in general?'

Bergan smiled up at him. 'Both. It's very nice to feel so…secure, but…' She stopped and shook her head.

'But what?'

'It's nothing.'

'Bergan?' There was a hint of amused exasperation in his voice.

'It's just this whole relationship thing. Whether or not we go slowly or speed on through like a freight train. It's still a relationship.'

'Is it the word that bothers you?'

'Perhaps.'

He nodded, his tone still calm and controlled. 'A friendship is a relationship. We enter into a relationship with our patients in a professional and medical capacity. There are many different types of relationships and you're fantastic at all of them.' He fixed her with a pointed look. '*All* of them.'

'Hmm.' She sounded as though she wasn't convinced and when she eased out from his arms he reluctantly released his hold. She walked over to the window.

'We're friends, Bergan. Or at least I'd like to think we are.'

She looked at him over her shoulder and nodded. 'Yes.'

'And friends like to spend time together, correct?'

'Yes.' She turned from the window and crossed her arms in front of her, giving him a studious look. It was one he'd seen plenty of times when she was pondering things. Good. It was good she was asking questions, trying to figure out the whys and wherefores of a healthy, normal courtship.

'Friends can hang out together, watch movies, discuss a variety of topics and sometimes they hug and hold hands, too.'

Her eyes widened a little, veiled fear behind them. 'So you're saying all you feel for me is friendship?' Her voice cracked on the final word and she immediately closed her eyes, not wanting him to see or worry about the internal turmoil that she'd done her best to keep locked up in the back of her mind. She'd tried not to put a definition on what they shared, but it was becoming more and more difficult to ignore it, especially when he didn't seem to want to make any move whatsoever to kiss her properly.

'No. I think you know I feel a lot more than that.'

'I also know that soon you'll be leaving Australia.'

'And returning to Paris.' He nodded, noting that she hadn't said 'leaving *me*'. 'This is a fact we've both been very aware of.' Richard wasn't quite sure what the problem was and as he took a few steps closer towards Bergan, she took one back, coming into contact with the window ledge.

She watched him slowly coming closer, his stance almost predatory but at the same time playful. She liked the combination. There was no anger, no abusive look in his eyes, only intrigue and interest.

'I like you, Bergan. A lot. I think I might have mentioned that once or twice before.'

'Uh-huh.' Where was her brain? Why did she feel the need to rebuild her protective walls when just last night she'd reclined on the lounge while he'd played an acoustic piece on his guitar? Her eyes had been closed, her body relaxed, her defences down as she'd absorbed the beautiful music he'd created with his clever hands. She'd been so open to him and now she wanted nothing more than to shut him out.

'So what's really the problem here?'

Bergan glanced away from him, unable to meet his powerful gaze, knowing sometimes that all it took was one look into his sexy eyes for her to lose all ability of rational thought. 'Noth—'

He stood before her and placed a finger across her lips.

'Don't say "nothing", because we both know it's not true. This is supposed to be an open and honest relationship and it works both ways. If you have anything you need to say to me, please, by all means, say it.'

There was a challenge in his words and she instantly raised her chin, a flash of defiance running through her eyes. 'All right, then. I guess...what's been bothering me has everything to do with why you never seem to want to kiss me. Not just on the cheek, but to...you know... properly... Oh, help.' She stopped, knowing she wasn't explaining succinctly enough.

'*Want* to kiss you?' Richard stared at her in bemusement, momentarily stunned. 'Of course I *want* to kiss you, Bergan. Why wouldn't you think I'd want that?'

'Well...because you haven't even *tried* to kiss me. I mean, I like the long and lingering kisses on my cheek at the end of a night together, but...' She stopped and closed her eyes for a moment.

'You're upset because I won't kiss you?' He gave his head a little shake, wanting to make sure he understood exactly what she was saying.

She looked up at him. 'Yes.' Not wanting to stand there that close to him when she felt this silly, she quickly sidestepped him and headed for the protection of her desk. She pulled back the executive chair but didn't sit down. Instead, she placed her fingertips on her desk and forced herself to slow down her breathing. 'And don't look at me like that.'

'Like what?' He spread both arms wide.

'Like you think I'm insane.'

His smile was immediate. 'I do not think you're insane, Bergan.'

'Yes, you do. I can see it in your eyes.'

Richard shook his head as he made his way towards her. 'It's not insanity you see there but incredulity.' He reached out and took both her hands in his. 'Don't you remember what I said to you when we first started changing our relationship? I said that I would wait for *you* to set the pace. That I would be a perfect gentleman—'

'Until I said otherwise? Letting me take all the responsibility, all the blame when it doesn't work out?' She dropped his hands and moved away, skirting round to the other side of the desk. She knew her actions were probably childish, but right now she didn't care. She was worried, stressed, completely out of her depth with the way this man was making her feel, and that was causing her to behave a little irrationally.

'No. Bergan?' He spread his arms wide again, his gaze imploring. 'Of course we both take responsibility.'

'And yet you're leaving. You're flying back to Paris.'

'Yes.' He still wasn't sure what the problem was.

'And…and you'll be surrounded by all those other French women, and…and…'

'Yes?' He wanted nothing more than to go to her, to pull her close, but he feared that if he moved yet again, chasing her around the office, she'd clam up and not tell him what was *really* wrong. He still wasn't sure where she was going with her little speech, but he wanted to be encouraging, to let her know he hadn't been toying with her emotions, as she was implying.

'And they're far more sophisticated and stunning than I will ever be.'

'*That's* what's bothering you?' Richard was gobsmacked.

Again she lifted her chin, that defiance in her eyes once more as though she was daring him to say something derogatory, something hurtful, something she could use to push him away. 'Yes.'

Richard closed his eyes for a second, pleased he'd managed to figure things out. She was upset because she was jealous. He never would have guessed, especially when she had no need of the emotion.

'Bergan.' He walked quickly round the desk and came towards her, instantly sliding his arms around her waist and drawing her close. She gasped at the suddenness of his movements but her shock soon turned to delight as she rested her hands against his chest.

'I don't know where this attraction between us might lead. I don't know what's going to happen when I get back to Paris, but I can tell you I'll be focused on my work, not on seeing how many Parisian women I can date.'

'I just thought that now that you've...you know, sort of broken your drought and started enjoying a relationship with me, that when you went back...' She stopped and closed her eyes. 'I sound ridiculous.'

'No. No, you don't,' he replied. 'I'm as much out of my depth as you are, but what I do know is that right here, right now, being with you, I'm happy. I won't make empty promises to you because at the moment my future's in limbo. I don't know what's going to happen once the fellowship's over, once I get back to my apartment, my work, my life in Paris.'

He looked away from her for a moment, but she'd seen the confusion in his eyes.

'I won't bring my uncertainty into your world, Bergan, especially when you've experienced so much uncertainty most of your life. All I am certain of, at the moment, is that being with you makes me happy and I haven't felt truly happy in a very long time.'

Bergan swallowed over the dryness in her throat, his words having affected her far more than she'd realised. Her heart was pounding against her chest, and she wanted him to know that she didn't expect a life plan from him, neither did she want definite answers to her questions, because even the thought of Richard telling her this thing that existed between them, this natural chemistry that had turned their worlds upside down in such a short space of time, wasn't going to last was enough to pierce her heart with pain.

'Is that why you haven't kissed me? Because you can't make any promises?' She forced her words into the room, needing to at least know the answer to that question.

'Oh, Bergan.' He lifted one hand to cup her cheek as he gazed down into her upturned face. 'As I've said before, *you* control how fast this relationship moves.' Gently, tenderly, he brushed his thumb over her plump lips. Bergan gasped, her lips instantly parting at the touch. Richard slid his other arm more firmly around her waist, drawing her close once more.

'If you want me to kiss you, all you have to do is say so.'

Bergan gazed up into his mesmerising blue eyes, knowing that even now, if she didn't say anything, he wouldn't push her. Here was a man who was desperate to continue proving to her that he was trustworthy, that he kept his word.

She still wasn't sure what was going to happen once he left Australia and returned to Paris. Would he forget her? Would he ever return? She shoved the thoughts back into their box, not wanting to deal with them but rather enjoy the man who was holding her close, looking at her as though she really was the most precious thing in the world.

'Kissing,' she said softly as she began to slide her hands up towards his neck, 'is very personal. It's powerful and it's far more important than people realise.' The instant the words were out of her mouth, the atmosphere between them seemed to intensify one hundred per cent. She continued to push forward, breaking through barriers she'd spent years erecting.

'Yes.' The word was barely a whisper and his parted lips didn't move. He simply continued to drink her in, the way she looked, the touch of her hands on his body, the way she was driving him completely insane.

'When two people touch their lips together, it's not about the pressure, it's not about the need. It's about two worlds melding into one. It's about giving and receiving in equal measure. It's about trust and honesty and belief.'

'Yes,' he repeated, but this time when he swallowed, her gaze dipped to watch his Adam's apple slide smoothly up and down his neck, just above his shirt collar and tie. The desire in him increased when he realised he might finally be able to follow through on the one thing he'd wanted to do since the moment he'd first seen her.

'Even with the anticipation of a kiss,' she continued, her soft words winding their way seductively around him, binding them together, 'bodies flood with desire, with longing, with a need so powerful it can make your head spin, make you swoon, wondering if your thirst will ever be quenched.'

'Yes.' The word was more of a soft growl, and although he had one hand at her waist and the other cupping her cheek, he still kept all his repressed desire perfectly contained.

'Yes,' she breathed, and stood on tiptoe, sliding her fingers around his neck and urging his head down so that finally, *finally*, their lips could meet.

# CHAPTER EIGHT

RICHARD KNEW HE had to remain calm and in control. Even though he was surging with elation at being invited by Bergan to kiss her, something he'd been longing to do for quite some time, the last thing he wanted was to scare her away. Enthusiasm was one thing, but unleashing his—

The phone on Bergan's desk shrilled to life, as did both their pagers. They could perhaps ignore one. They certainly couldn't ignore all three. Richard still kept his arm around her waist, not wanting to let her go but knowing, eventually, he must.

'Hold that thought,' she said, pressing a kiss to her finger and then placing her finger gently on his lips. Smiling, she turned and reached across her desk to answer the phone. 'Dr Moncrief,' she said into the receiver. 'All right. Give me the details.' She shuffled around her desk and quickly picked up a pen to jot down a few notes.

'I'll be right out,' she said a moment later, then paused and looked up at Richard. 'I'm sure Richard's not too far away, especially as his shift has already started.' With that, she rang off.

'Why didn't you say I was in here with you?' he asked as she picked up the piece of paper she'd scribbled notes on and headed for the door. 'It's hardly uncommon for the two of us to talk in private.'

'I just don't like everyone knowing my business.' Her words were sharper than she'd intended but instead of apologising she switched her mind into professional mode. 'Besides, duty calls. A building has collapsed downtown.'

'Good heavens!' Richard was shocked. 'What are the preliminary details?'

'A heritage-listed building, three stories, used as professional rooms.' She looked at the piece of paper in her hand as they headed into A and E. She'd had half a mind to ask him to wait a few minutes so no one saw them heading into A and E together but he'd been right. There was no reason why it would seem odd if the two of them were alone in her office.

She'd overreacted when Katrina, the triage sister, had mentioned being unable to find Dr Allington and had blurted out the first thing that had come to mind. She wasn't used to being flustered about her personal life, primarily because prior to meeting Richard she hadn't really had one.

'There you both are,' Katrina said as they entered the nurses' station. The phones were ringing, several nurses telling the staff who had been called in about the latest emergency requiring the Sunshine General retrieval team to assemble. 'Here's the latest report from the police, who have not long arrived on the scene.'

Bergan scanned the information.

'What's the suspected headcount?' Richard asked.

She looked up at him for a moment, seemingly not having heard him, but after a moment she returned her attention to the sheet. 'In excess of twenty, possibly up to fifty. The building housed the offices of a lawyer, doctor and dentist.'

'Any preliminary conclusions about the cause of the collapse? Burst water mains? Gas explosion? Bad foundations?'

Bergan scanned the report and then nodded. 'Fire crews

suspect a gas explosion.' She glanced at him again. 'Have you...been involved in a retrieval like this before?'

'Unfortunately, yes. Buildings may not collapse every day but, yes, I've been involved with this sort of retrieval in the past.'

'Good. Well, if you have any tips,' she said as quite a few of the retrieval team started to gather in the nurses' station, 'don't be afraid to speak up.'

'Oh, I will.' Richard gave her one of those small smiles that never failed to make her heart flip-flop. She wished he wouldn't, especially now when she was trying desperately to concentrate and put what they'd been so close to finally achieving back there in her office completely out of her mind. It wasn't like her to be so unprofessional, but there it was—she was affected by him even in the midst of a crisis. Surely that wasn't right?

Once the majority of the retrieval team had arrived, Bergan accepted the latest updated information from Katrina, who had just finished a phone call from a police officer on the scene, and began the briefing, pleased that her friends, Mackenzie, Reggie and Sunainah, each qualified specialists in their own right, would also make up part of the team heading out to the accident site.

'We've contacted the Red Cross and they'll be setting up a temporary triage station at the local community hall, which is only half a block down from the collapsed building,' Bergan stated. 'Katrina and Sunainah, I'd like you to go there and work with the volunteers to get things set up as quickly as possible. At the moment the count is at least thirty people trapped in the collapsed building, but that doesn't take into account patients or clients who may have been in the waiting rooms of the three different businesses.'

She looked across at Sunainah. 'The dentist's rooms

were holding a school clinic today, which is why I'll need you there as lead paediatrician,' she told her friend.

Sunainah nodded in acceptance and Bergan continued. 'The collapse has also affected traffic. Several chunks of the building have fallen onto the footpath and the road so we could be looking at more than sixty possible patients. Some might have scratches and bruises, but others will definitely need more treatment. Extra staff have been called into A and E and both emergency and elective theatres are preparing for the influx.'

'I take it the police have cordoned off the entire block?' Richard asked.

'But we still have access to the community centre?' Mackenzie checked.

'Yes.' As Bergan continued to give out jobs and direct her team, she couldn't help being highly conscious of Richard standing just off to her right. As she looked around at the staff, some already dressed in their bright blue and yellow retrieval overalls, she tried to avoid looking directly at Richard. Just the sight of his bluer-than-blue eyes, eyes that were so expressive they had the ability to make her knees turn to jelly with one simple look, was enough to ruin her concentration.

She'd been about to kiss him. To really kiss him! She'd dreamt of it often enough during the past few weeks, and while she'd been delighted that he hadn't pressured her, that he'd let her set the pace, she honestly hadn't expected him to hold back as much as he had. Had he honestly been waiting for her to give him permission to kiss her? That in itself spoke volumes about his character, about his trustworthiness, about how he was showing her she could rely on him to stay true to his word.

Bergan had given up years ago ever thinking a man like Richard Allington existed. A man who *was* honourable, giving and caring. He often treated her as though she were some sort of queen, his considerate nature showing her that he wanted nothing more than to make her happy. Was it possible? *Could* she allow herself to be happy? Not just for now but for *ever*?

She made the mistake of glancing at him just as she started to wrap up her instructions, and at the serious look of concentration on his face Bergan once again felt her heart melt. He cared. He really cared about his work, about people, about the patients they were about to go and help. And he really cared about her, too.

For so long she'd kept her heart wrapped up tight, locked behind imaginary doors, knowing if she went to great lengths to protect herself, no one could ever hurt her again. And they hadn't. She was a strong, proud and very independent woman, but when she was alone with Richard, especially sharing a quiet night just sitting and chatting, or watching a television show with his arm securely around her as she snuggled into him, Bergan had to admit she felt happy and feminine but also incredibly vulnerable…and it was the last part she didn't like.

'What about me?' Richard asked. 'You haven't given me a job yet. Floating between the site and the community centre?'

'No. You have experience with this type of rescue, so you'll be with me.' She cleared her throat as she said the last words then nodded to everyone else gathered around her. 'That's about it.' As people started to disband, to go and do as she'd instructed, Bergan called out, 'And don't forget to ensure your walkie-talkies are switched to the right frequency.'

She let out a long sigh as she turned to face Richard, who was now leaning against the desk.

'How are you holding up?' he asked.

'OK.'

'Retrievals are never easy—emotionally, I mean. I think that's when we all really need be totally professional in order to deal with the unusual situation we're walking into.'

'Yes.'

'You do very well, preparing the staff, giving everyone jobs. Holding it all together.' He nodded. 'You're an expert at that.'

Bergan frowned. 'Is that a back-handed compliment?'

'What?' Richard looked surprised. 'No. Of course it isn't. I'm saying I admire you, Bergan. I almost envy the way you're able to keep it all together.'

She shifted her weight to the other foot and crossed her arms, looking him directly in the eye. 'Are you saying you can't?'

He stood up straight, giving her a quizzical glance. 'What's wrong? Why are you being so antagonistic towards me?' His words weren't rude, just confused, and Bergan didn't blame him. It wasn't fair of her to snap at him simply because he had the ability to break through her barriers, to get her excited, to make her feel vulnerable.

'Nothing.' She closed her eyes for a second and shook her head. 'I'd better get changed.' Without waiting for a reply, Bergan headed off towards the female change rooms, leaving a very confused Richard watching her walk away.

When they arrived at the accident site, the police waved through the mini-van carrying the staff and the two ambulances that had come to take the first of the injured back to the hospital. The members of the team began to disperse, each one knowing exactly what to do and where he or she was needed.

'Bergan.' A man dressed in a firefighter's rescue uniform came up to her.

'Palmer. I was told you were the man in charge of everything. Good.' She jerked her thumb over her shoulder. 'This is Richard Allington. We'll be working point with you at the site.'

'Terry Palmer,' the man said, and quickly shook hands with Richard, before leading the two of them through the maze of police cars and fire trucks towards the rubble that had previously been a place of business.

'Status update?' Bergan and Richard both carried large medical kits as they followed Palmer, taking in the sight of destruction as well as the smell of despair and devastation.

'You couldn't have timed it better. We're about to pull the first of the survivors from the rubble. There are several pedestrians and motorists who require medical attention, but now that your teams are here, they'll no doubt take care of them.'

'That's what they're trained to do,' Bergan replied as she navigated around a large section of broken sandstone. 'It was reported as a gas explosion.'

'That's the preliminary finding but we won't know for sure until later. At this point we've taken the necessary precautions and shut down all non-essential services to this area.'

'And the community centre?' Richard asked. 'I understand that's close by. Does it have water?'

'Yes. Also, it doesn't have gas pipes, it's all electric, so the medical teams and the Red Cross volunteers should be able to do what needs to be done.'

Bergan continued to look around them as they drew closer to the centre of the blast. 'Oh, my goodness!' she gasped, placing her free hand over her mouth, more from shock at what she was seeing than to protect herself from the dust cloud, which seemed to be suspended in the air.

The actual site looked more like an anthill than a building. Several of Palmer's men, in their bright reflective yellow clothes, were clambering on the mound, carefully moving pieces of rubble with their gloved hands, while others where setting up the heavier machinery that would be required to lift the large sections.

'It doesn't matter how many times you see it, you're never fully prepared for the devastation.' Richard placed his hand on her shoulder, giving it a little reassuring squeeze, showing her he understood exactly how she was feeling. It was strange how alike they were, how they seemed to think the same. It was another thing she wasn't quite used to, having a man actually understand the way she thought.

'Palmer!' one of the firefighters called, and immediately Palmer went over, scrambling over the rubble as easily as a mountain goat. A moment later Palmer was calling them over.

Richard and Bergan made their way towards him and by the time they arrived, one young girl, about eleven years old with braces on her teeth, was being lifted carefully onto a stretcher.

'Where do you want her?' the firefighter asked.

Bergan quickly looked around, her mind snapping into professional mode, and pointed to a more level part of the rubble. 'Just there. Let me assess her.'

'We've got another one,' one of the men called, and Richard only had to glance at Bergan for them to communicate effectively what needed to be done. She knelt down by the young girl and opened her medical kit as Richard went off to attend to the next patient. They both knew that the sooner people were pulled from the rubble and treated, the better the outcome.

By the time Bergan had dealt with the young girl, calling through on her walkie-talkie to alert Sunainah to the first paediatric case, another patient was waiting for her.

'We've managed to move a large section of the brickwork, which has thankfully given us access to what used to be the dentist's area,' Palmer told her as she dispatched an elderly man back to Sunshine General in an ambulance. 'Once we've sorted out this section, we can start heading downwards, picking our way carefully.'

'How long will it take to clear the whole site?'

'Could be as long as a day or two. It just depends.'

Bergan pursed her lips, but at the call of another person being lifted from the mound of despair she nodded and headed over to do her job. The next woman to be extracted had multiple fractures to her legs and arms and Bergan immediately radioed for Mackenzie's orthopaedic expertise.

'How are things at the community centre?' she asked her friend as the two of them worked together after Mackenzie had joined her, Bergan inserting an intravenous drip into the woman's arm as Mackenzie splinted the woman's legs.

'Settled.' Mackenzie shrugged. 'Quite a few people being treated for shock, unable to believe something like this could happen in downtown Maroochydore. Where's Richard?' she asked.

Bergan looked around their immediate vicinity, but there was no sign of him. 'I haven't seen him for quite a while. He'll be around somewhere. I'll check with Palmer.'

'Right. I can take it from here. Is there an ambulance due back soon?'

'One is expected in about five minutes.'

'Excellent.'

Bergan left Mackenzie with the patient and headed over to where Palmer was talking to someone on his walkie-talkie. He stood near the edge of one of the large holes that had been excavated. There were also a few abseiling ropes going down into the hole, indicating there were men down there, working their hardest to continue rescuing people from the rubble.

'Status update? Over.' Palmer waited for a moment and Bergan listened in, waiting to ask Palmer if he knew where Richard had gone.

'Slow, but we can hear her and she can hear us. Over.'

'That's Richard!' Bergan stated with incredulity, and pointed to the walkie-talkie in Palmer's hand.

'Yes.'

'What's he doing down there?' And why was there a sudden weight pressing on her chest? Concern for his safety, the need to see with her own eyes that he was indeed OK became paramount. She closed her eyes for a brief moment, trying to get her thoughts under control, to pull on her professionalism, but all she saw was the image of Richard lying in that large hole, covered with dust and rubble. She swallowed convulsively, unable to stop the sensation of dread spreading through her. At a loud noise from down in the hole, her eyes snapped open and she stared worriedly at Palmer.

'Is he all right? Is Richard all right?'

Palmer frowned at her for a second, clearly puzzled by her reaction, before nodding. 'He's fine. There's a woman down there who my men have been talking to while they dig her out. She was complaining of pain and they were hoping that if they could at least get one of her limbs exposed, Richard might be able to put a drip in.' Palmer shrugged. 'Whether or not they'll succeed in time is anybody's guess, but we need to be prepared.'

'I quite agree, but—' She stopped, almost about to ask Palmer why it had to be *Richard* who had gone down, but of course she knew the answer. He was not only a brilliant doctor with experience in such situations, but she also had no doubt that he'd volunteered for the task. It was just like him. Part of her was proud of his courage, the other part was frightened in case something bad happened.

'Is it stable?' she asked Palmer, and to her surprise there was a tremor in her voice. 'The walls, I mean. They won't cave in?'

'It's safe, Bergan. I wouldn't let my men down there if it wasn't. You know what a safety-first type of guy I am.'

She nodded, knowing he spoke the truth. They'd worked together on different retrievals quite a lot over the years, and even though she'd politely refused his suggestions that they perhaps turn their professional relationship into something more, she still knew she could rely on Palmer never to put anyone in danger.

Palmer's walkie-talkie crackled and one of his men spoke.

'We're getting closer but the doc thinks he might need assistance with the medical stuff. Is there anyone free up there to give him a hand? Over.'

'I'll do it,' Bergan volunteered, before Palmer could depress the button to reply. When he looked at her, she shrugged. 'I know how to abseil and I am currently without a patient to care for.'

Palmer nodded. 'Bergan will be down in a few minutes. Over.'

With that, she walked over to where the harnesses were kept and stepped into one, buckling it securely. Palmer hooked her into a D-clamp and attached the ropes, handing her a pair of gloves. 'I don't know if they're a good fit. They might be a bit big.'

She slipped her hands in. 'I'll manage.'

'You always do.' Palmer double-checked her ropes and clamps, before announcing to his men that she was on her way down.

Taking a deep breath, Bergan eased over the edge of the

rubble before seating herself more firmly into the harness. Slowly feeding the rope through the clamp, she lowered herself into the hole, looking down towards the shining lights the workers had set up.

'Almost there,' she heard Richard's voice say, and in another few moments she felt his hands clamp around her waist to steady her until her feet met the uneven ground. She turned to face him, their hard hats almost hitting each other. 'Good of you to drop in,' he murmured, and some of the men chuckled.

'She's down. Over.' Richard spoke into the walkie-talkie, then helped to unhook her from the abseiling rope. Bergan pulled off her gloves, her gaze travelling over Richard as though to reassure herself that he was indeed OK. She let out a sigh of relief, her mind beginning to clear of the fog that had surrounded it.

'Status?' she asked, pleased to feel more in control, more like her old self again.

'Female, thirty-one years old. Wendy. Married with one child, who has already been lifted out. She's conscious, quite lucid, can't feel her legs, is having trouble breathing and is very dizzy.' Richard spoke quietly as he led Bergan carefully towards where the men were still excavating.

'Prognosis?'

Richard met her gaze and as her eyes had now had time to adjust to the change from natural to artificial light, she could see the pain reflected there as he slowly shook his head. 'It's not good. I don't know how we're going to sit there, talking to her, waiting patiently for the rescue team to dig her out, but—'

'That's our job,' she finished for him. She could feel his fear for the patient, but was amazed at the way he was able to hold himself together.

She slipped her hand into his and gave it a reassuring

squeeze. 'You're not alone, Richard. Whatever it is we need to face, we can face it together.'

As she spoke the words, looking up into his eyes, she realised she truly meant those words, not just in relation to their present situation. She *wanted* to be with Richard. She *wanted* to support him and to have him support her in return. She *wanted* to face whatever life threw at them and she wanted them to face it…together.

# CHAPTER NINE

'HELLO? RICHARD? ARE you still there?' a woman's voice asked.

Richard cleared his throat as Wendy's voice floated up through the rubble. He let go of Bergan's hand and with extreme caution sat down on the pile of bricks and mortar near where Wendy's voice had come from. Bergan followed suit.

'I'm still here, Wendy.' To Bergan's surprise, his tone was calm and controlled. 'Just helping my colleague down.'

'Oh. Is that Bergan?' Wendy's voice was interested and Bergan frowned for a moment, feeling a little strange at meeting a woman she couldn't see.

'You told her about me?' Bergan's words were a quiet, perplexed whisper and whether it was the surprised look on her face or the fact that he really was drawing strength from her, Richard nodded his head and smiled.

'How could I not?' he said softly, then angled his head towards the rubble. 'Talk to her. Help me help her.'

Bergan nodded and cleared her throat. 'I'm here, too, Wendy. Can you tell me how you're feeling?'

There was a moment of silence before Wendy's wavering words floated up to them. 'I can't feel my legs.' The sentence ended with a sob and Bergan raised her gaze to look at Richard, communicating wordlessly that this probably meant there was some sort of spinal damage.

'What about your hands? Can you wriggle your fingers?'

'Yes. I can wriggle my fingers on my left hand, but it really hurts when I try to do it on the right.'

'Possible fractured arm.' Richard spoke softly.

Bergan nodded. 'What about your head?'

'I'm dizzy.'

'That's natural.' Bergan tried to inject a calmness into her tone she didn't really feel. The one thing they had to do at the moment was to keep Wendy as reassured and as stable as possible. 'Talk to her for a moment,' she said to Richard as she held out her free hand for the walkie-talkie. 'I need to give Palmer instructions.' Richard started talking to Wendy while Bergan called up to Palmer.

'I want Reggie and Mackenzie at the top of the hole with a waiting ambulance as soon as we're ready to bring Wendy up. No excuses. Over.' There was determination in her tone. They were going to get Wendy out and she was going to be alive when they did.

With Reggie and Mackenzie waiting at the top, Wendy would be guaranteed two of the best surgeons Sunshine General employed. Bergan pushed aside the small bubble of doubt that entered her thoughts as she glanced at the workers who were carefully and as quickly as possible removing the rubble that had buried Wendy. They *would* get Wendy out—alive.

'I think Mackenzie went back to the hospital with a patient. Over.'

'I said no excuses. You tell them *I* need them. Use those exact words. That'll be enough. Over.' Bergan placed the walkie-talkie in Richard's top overall pocket. 'Let's get set up.'

'Richard? Bergan?' Wendy's words floated up. 'What's… what's happening?'

There was a smile in Richard's voice as he spoke. 'Bergan's switching into stubborn mode.'

'Is that a good thing?' Wendy wanted to know.

Richard's rich chuckle filled the cavern as he watched Bergan open the medical kit and start preparing what they'd need for an intravenous drip. He noted she had both a bag of saline and a bag of plasma. 'That's a very good thing, Wendy. Never have I met a more stubborn woman than Bergan.'

'Really?' Bergan was surprised at that. 'Never? You've worked all over the world and you've never met a woman more stubborn than me?' She kept her tone light but loud enough for Wendy to hear.

'I speak the truth,' Richard remarked.

'You two sound like you're much closer than just colleagues.' Wendy's words floated up to them and Bergan could hear that she was definitely interested. That was good. If they could keep Wendy's cognitive functions working, keep her lucid until they could reach her, that would be fantastic.

'When you work closely with people, you tend to build closer relationships,' Bergan stated, needing to keep her words matter-of-fact because if she stopped to think about the personal relationship she presently shared with Richard, she might lose her focus altogether. 'Wendy, can you tell me where it hurts most?' she asked.

Bergan was determined to do everything in her power to save Wendy's life. She wasn't sure exactly *how* she was going to accomplish that but she'd learned long ago that if she focused her determination, if she dug her stubborn heels into a situation, she could usually make some sort of difference.

'Wendy? Wendy?' she called when the other woman didn't reply instantly. 'Where does it hurt?'

'Everywhere. My stomach. My heart. My head.'

Bergan closed her eyes, trying to picture Wendy's body, trying to get a clear picture in her mind so that when they had access, she could work more quickly. 'Try and be specific. I know it's not easy, Wendy, but when we get to you—'

'If,' Wendy interrupted.

'*When* we get to you,' Bergan said, stubborn determination in her voice. 'It will make it easier for Richard and I if we know more about where the pain is centred. Just try and focus for me, Wendy. We are going to get you out and you are going to live. I want you to believe that and if you can't believe, I want you to believe in Richard and me. I want you to believe in the crews that are working so incredibly hard up here to make sure we get to you very, very soon.

'I want you to believe that I have two of my best friends, two women who are brilliant surgeons, waiting for you at the top, to give you the treatment you need so you can recover and get back to your family. This *is* possible, Wendy, and as difficult as it is right now to hang on to hope…' Bergan looked across at Richard, who had pulled on a pair of heavy gloves and was helping the crews lift a particularly large section of bricks. He seemed to feel her eyes on him and the instant their gazes met, Bergan said, 'There always has to be hope.'

'She's right,' one of the rescue workers said, and Bergan was amazed to see their weary bodies almost flood with energy, flood with strength, even though they'd already been working so hard for so long.

'Wendy?' Bergan called. 'Where does it hurt?'

'It hurts most near my stomach and I…I keep getting very dizzy and…and tired,' Wendy said, sniffing a little, then coughing and moaning in pain. Bergan closed her eyes, forcing herself to concentrate, drawing a mental picture of Wendy's situation. Opening her eyes, she pulled a few more things to the front of the medical kit, ensuring she would have everything she needed at her fingertips.

'I can see her!' The call came from one of the rescue workers who was lying down on his stomach, peering through a small crack in the rubble. 'Not too far below us is another cavern, similar to this one, so we're going to need to go slowly so we don't cause a cave-in, but I can see her.'

The words were like another burst of energy for the crews, one of them radioing up to Palmer to let him know of this latest development.

Richard and Bergan quickly picked up their equipment and carefully made their way around to where the worker was lying on his stomach.

'Where?' Bergan asked, and as he shifted, she lay down and peered through the hole, surprised that Wendy was indeed much closer than she'd originally thought. She could see the left side of Wendy's body and it was then she realised the woman was lying at an angle, a large wooden beam pinning down the lower half of her body and broken bricks pressing into her back, as well as her abdomen. The woman's face, however, was partly obscured from view.

'Wendy. Wendy, we can see you!' She shifted out of the way so Richard could look and also assess the situation.

'Really?' Wendy instantly tried to shift at this news. It was a natural human reaction.

'Stay still,' Richard instructed. 'It's natural to want to move but we need you to remain as still and as calm as you have been up until now. You're doing an incredible job, Wendy,' Richard said encouragingly as he straightened. 'How is she breathing?' he asked softly, looking at Bergan.

'There must be a pocket of air around her mouth and nose,' Bergan guessed with a shrug of her shoulders. 'Whatever it is, I'm not going to quibble because it's allowed her enough oxygen to stay alive.'

'Good point.' Richard nodded then angled his words down towards Wendy's body. 'The crews up here are going to do their thing while Bergan and I get ready. Just remember to stay as still as possible.'

'OK.' The hope in her tone was obvious. Until then, it had been difficult to keep the other woman's spirits buoyed, but they'd done it and now they were going to get her out.

As the crews continued to work, Bergan asked Wendy about her family, about her husband and children, because now that Wendy had hope, she was happy to talk about those who would hopefully be seeing her soon.

With crews that were galvanised into action, with Bergan and Richard standing ready and Palmer radioing that both Mackenzie and Reggie, as well as the ambulance, were waiting for them at the top, the rescue seemed to speed up. A stretcher was lowered down via abseiling ropes, ready and waiting for Wendy.

'How much longer until we can get to her?' Bergan asked, hating that all they could do at the moment was wait. It was the part of being out on retrieval she hated most. She wanted to pace up and down, but that was impossible in their present circumstances. As her impatient agitation increased, Richard placed both hands on her shoulders and forced her to look at him.

'Settle. Calm. Breathe.'

'I can't. I need to be next to Wendy, treating her, making a difference, doing *something*.' She shook her head.

'I know, but it won't be too much longer.' He rubbed his hands up and down her upper arms, wanting to support her. 'The fact that each second feels as long as a minute doesn't help either.'

'No.'

'Bergan? Richard?' one of the rescuers called. 'We've managed to open the cavern a bit.'

'We have access to her?'

'We do. Her left arm is clear, so at least you can start to treat her now.'

'That's marvellous news.'

Richard and Bergan carefully made their way across the rubble to where a new area had been excavated.

'You go first,' Richard said. 'You're much lighter than I am. I can pass you what you need.'

'OK.'

The rescuers were talking to Wendy, keeping her lucid, but when Bergan spoke she could almost hear the relief in Wendy's tone.

'I thought you'd left me,' the woman said, a quiver in her voice.

'Not a chance,' Bergan replied as she followed the instructions given by the crew to sit down and carefully slide and crawl her way closer to Wendy.

'The last thing we want is for that pile to shift.'

'Agreed.'

'Wendy?' Bergan spoke softly once she was in position.

'You're here?' Wendy's tone was filled with excited relief.

'I am. I'm going to touch your free arm now.' Bergan reached out a gloved hand and placed it on Wendy's right arm. 'I know this is going to be very difficult, given we're so close to getting you out, but we still need to take everything very slowly, to take our time, to make sure nothing goes wrong. And to do that I need you to be as still as possible.'

She found the pulse at Wendy's wrist and did a quick count of the beats. 'Sphygmo,' she said to Richard, who instantly nodded and located the portable sphygmomanometer in the medical kit.

Bergan shone the torchlight onto Wendy's arm, hoping to find a decent vein, one that could easily house a needle, which would be connected to a bag of plasma. 'I want to try and talk you through everything I'm doing so you're not startled. The last thing we want right now is to startle you and cause you to move suddenly.'

'Yes.'

'I'm going to wind a cuff around your arm so I can take your blood pressure. All right?'

'Yes,' Wendy replied again.

'After that, from what you've been telling me, with the way you've been feeling dizzy and sometimes zoning in and out, there's a high probability that you're bleeding internally. So what I want to do is first of all give you something for the pain and then I'll put a needle into your arm. That will be attached to a bag of plasma, which will help keep your blood level more stable. The more we can do for you down here, the more stable you'll be when you're ready to go to Theatre.'

'OK.' Wendy was silent for a moment. 'Is Richard near?'

'I'm here, Wendy,' he responded as he accepted the sphygmo back from Bergan. They'd been working alongside each other in the A and E for a couple of weeks now so she wasn't surprised at the way he was able to pre-empt everything she required.

'Of course you want him to talk to you.' Bergan chuckled. 'He has a much sexier voice than mine.'

'I guess he does,' Wendy agreed, and there was a clear hint of embarrassment along with appreciation in her tone. 'But that doesn't mean I don't want to hear yours.'

'Well, I appreciate that,' Bergan said as she drew up an injection of methoxyflurane for pain relief. 'I'm going to swab your arm and give you an injection. You may feel even more light-headed afterwards, but keep trying to talk to us, all right?'

'I'll try.'

'Good.' Bergan administered the injection, then explained to Wendy how she was going to set up the intravenous drip. Throughout it all the crews continued to work, Palmer kept calling down on the walkie-talkie for an update of the situation and little by little more of Wendy's body was exposed.

Finally, they were able to see Wendy's face, although the woman's legs were still trapped beneath the beam.

'We'll need to hook it to the winch to lift it off. Over,' one of the workers was telling Palmer. Things were definitely progressing but Bergan was more focused on Wendy's physical and emotional health. She fitted an oxygen non-rebreather mask over Wendy's mouth and nose, glad she and Richard were able to help the poor woman in whatever way they could. Although conditions were far from ideal, the fact they'd been able to get to Wendy as soon as possible could make a tremendous difference.

'There's a large gash on her abdomen,' Richard said, as one of the workers removed another piece of rubble, allowing him further access to Wendy's battered body. Richard shifted forward, carefully dragging the medical kit with him. He pulled on a fresh pair of gloves and reached for the heavy-duty scissors. He cut away Wendy's bloodstained and filthy clothing before reaching for some gauze. Bergan helped Richard clean the area around the long gash, debriding it carefully.

Richard glanced up at the area where the workers were carefully removing the rubble from near Wendy's face, pleased Bergan had already given her something for pain. 'How are you doing there, Wendy?'

'OK.'

'Let us know if you have any additional pain, OK? That's very important,' Richard said, as he carefully packed a sterile dressing into the wound, soaking up some of the blood so he could take a better look. 'I need someone to hold a torch for me,' he called, and one of the rescue workers was there within a matter of seconds, shining a bright overhead light onto Wendy's wound. 'Bergan, retract and repack,' he said, as she removed the bloodied packing and pulled the skin back with a retractor to afford Richard a better look.

'See anything?' she asked, also having a careful look.

'Aha.' He reached for a set of locking forceps and clamped the artery.

'I'll clean it up a little more,' Bergan said, packing the wound once more with clean gauze in order to give them the opportunity of a better look. Then she assisted Richard with suturing the offending artery.

'That should hold things for a while,' he stated as he gathered up the rubbish bag they'd been using. Bergan thanked the rescue worker for holding the torch as she put a firm bandage over the gash.

'How are you feeling now?' she asked as Wendy lay there, her eyes closed, her breathing calm beneath the oxygen mask.

'Floaty.'

Bergan smiled. 'Pain level?'

'OK.'

Bergan's tone was clear but firm as she and Richard continued to monitor the intravenous drip as well as regularly performing neurological observations. They began cleaning and debriding other wounds as soon as they could get to them.

Bergan once more checked Wendy's pupils, pleased things were progressing smoothly. Now, though, it was important Wendy understand the reality of her injuries, and while the information wouldn't be easy to hear, Bergan had learnt of old that it was best to deliver bad news as straightforwardly and with as much compassion as possible.

'Wendy, the damage to your legs is quite extensive.' Bergan watched Wendy's eyes and it was clear to see the anguish reflected there at the news. The poor woman. Bergan's heart went out to her.

'Yes,' she responded, her words barely audible behind the oxygen mask.

Bergan glanced over at Richard, their gazes meeting and holding. She could see he was just as affected by the situation as she was and it made her relax a little. Usually she had no trouble engaging her professional self, keeping her emotional distance from her patients so that she could do her job effectively. This time, with the heightened circumstances, it was little wonder she was feeling more vulnerable.

Richard gave her an encouraging nod, urging her to continue explaining things to Wendy while he continued to monitor her vital signs. The winch was being lowered and soon they'd have the large beam off Wendy's legs. Then things would move fast. They would need to assess, debride and possibly splint and bandage her legs as quickly as possible. It was clear the femoral artery hadn't been severed, otherwise Wendy would have bled out quite a while ago. But the extent of her fractures…? At this stage, it was anyone's guess.

'Mackenzie is the name of the orthopaedic surgeon who will be treating you. She'll discuss all the options with you once she knows what the damage is, but at this stage it doesn't look good. You can trust her, Wendy. She and I have been friends since we were kids.' Bergan shifted closer to Wendy and after removing her glove placed one hand on Wendy's shoulder as the woman closed her eyes and let the tears quietly flow. Bergan had to bite her lip and look away, otherwise she was in grave danger of losing it herself.

'Will I walk again?' Wendy wanted to know.

Bergan shook her head. 'It's too soon to give a firm diagnosis, but that is one possibility.'

'Not much longer now.' Richard's smooth voice was quiet, intimate, and when Bergan looked across at him, she saw he'd shifted closer, too. He removed one of his gloves and placed his hand over hers, the two of them wanting to show Wendy they supported her, but at the same time Bergan knew it was Richard's way of encouraging her. He was amazing.

Even as the thought passed through her mind, warning bells began to ring. He was amazing. He was supportive. He was handsome. He was kind. He was protective. He was giving. In short, Richard Allington was everything she'd ever allowed herself to dream about.

Naturally, these dreams had been carefully controlled and usually came out of the box she kept them in only when she was at her lowest of low points, wanting a knight in shining armour to ride up on his white horse and rescue her from her horrible life. Then, when she'd come to her senses, she'd push those dreams back into their box, telling herself sternly that no man like that even existed, let alone would come to rescue her.

Keeping people—and especially men—at a distance was one of her specialities, but somehow in a short time Richard had pushed through those barriers, broken them down little by little. In a way it was wonderful, liberating, but Bergan also knew it would end. Richard would leave her, return to Paris to his former life, and soon he would have forgotten all about her. The thought made her want to hold on tighter to him now, to never let him go—but she knew she must, and the sooner, the better.

He was her dream man. Very real and very difficult to resist. The fact that she was coming to rely on him, that she felt exposed and vulnerable around him, that she'd even contemplated spending the rest of her life with him, was enough to turn the warning bells into a full-blown air-raid siren inside her head.

Danger! *Danger!* She had to get away from him as quickly as possible, because if she didn't, when he left her—as she knew he would—she'd be the one with the broken heart.

# CHAPTER TEN

EVEN AFTER THEY'D managed to remove the beam from Wendy's legs then stabilise her and move her carefully onto a stretcher, Bergan still hadn't been able to shake the feeling that she was swimming in uncharted waters.

They handed Wendy's care over to Reggie and Mackenzie, who both went with her in the ambulance.

'What's next?' Bergan asked Palmer once she and Richard were up top again.

'There's not much else you can do here now. From the numbers the police have given us, we've managed to get everyone else out. Most have been sent to the community centre, although quite a few have been taken immediately to Sunshine General.'

'OK, thanks, Palmer.'

Palmer looked from Richard back to Bergan and nodded. 'You two make a good team.' He held out his hand to Richard and shook it. 'Take care of her.'

Richard shook Palmer's hand, looking as though he had no clue what was happening. 'Bergan takes pretty good care of herself.'

Bergan glanced up at Richard, pleased he'd championed her. He truly believed in her. The knowledge warmed her heart and at the same time only made it more difficult for her to distance herself from him.

'What was that all about?' Richard asked as they both walked away from the rubble.

Bergan shrugged. 'Nothing much.'

'Has he tried to date you in the past?'

'He's asked me out a few times.'

'Ah. He wants to protect you, eh?' Richard nodded. 'That makes more sense.'

'What do you mean?'

Richard pushed his hands through his hair a few times, glad the hard hat was off his head as he tried to shake out the dust, which no doubt made him look almost grey. 'Most men want to protect the women they're interested in, especially when they abseil into unstable caverns.'

Bergan frowned. 'So you're saying I shouldn't have abseiled down to help you out?' Her tone was clipped and instantly defensive.

Richard was astonished and placed a hand on her arm to stop her from walking. 'No.' He looked down into her face, wanting to make sure he conveyed his point as clearly as possible. 'As I said to Palmer, you can take care of yourself. It's quite evident you've been taking care of yourself for most of your life. All I meant was that a lot of men want to protect the women they care about. It's been going on since caveman days.'

He smiled at her, that gorgeous heart-thumping smile that never failed to send Bergan's insides into overdrive. How was it he could defuse her temper so easily? One moment she was hot under the collar and the next she was melting simply because he'd smiled!

She closed her eyes for a moment and shook her head, and a small smattering of dust came loose. Richard coughed and she looked up at him. 'Sorry,' she murmured, as he reached out and brushed his fingers lightly over her hair. She'd wound the long plait into a bun at the nape of her neck when she'd changed into her retrieval overalls, but, even having worn the hard hat, there was still dust everywhere.

'We look like an old grey-haired couple with all this dust.' He coughed again then chuckled, resting his hands on her shoulders. Without another word he pulled her close into his arms and rested his chin on her head. Bergan found herself going willingly, wanting to be held by him, wanting to feel those big strong arms around her.

It was wonderful and she desperately wanted it to last for ever, to know that Richard would always be there, right by her side, but…that wasn't her life and she knew it. She'd known it for as long as she could remember. She was not the sort of woman who was destined to live a normal life.

'Richard?' she said after a few moments.

'Mmm?'

'Do *you* want to protect me?'

He eased back and looked at her, his arms still firmly around her body. He stared into her eyes for a long moment and Bergan began to wonder if he was ever going to answer her. Finally, he cleared his throat. 'Of course I do.' More than she could possibly know, but the last thing he wanted was to scare her, to make her feel as though he was trying to change her. She'd opened up to him, she'd allowed him into her inner sanctum, but he could also sense there was something jittery about her. Whether that had anything to do with Wendy's rescue or something Palmer might have said, he had no idea.

'Don't *you* want to protect *me*?' he asked her, and for some reason she seemed surprised by the question.

'Well, do you need protecting?'

His smile was slow, sensual and incredibly sexy. 'Everyone needs protecting from something, Bergan.'

'What do you need protecting from?'

'Right now? I need protecting from moving too fast,

from wanting to capture your perfect lips in a perfect kiss—a kiss that has been a long time coming.' The last thing he wanted was to make a mistake, to do something that would spook Bergan, causing her to retreat.

'Why do you say things like that?' Bergan couldn't believe the slight tremble in her voice.

'Because I only want there to be truth between us.' He rubbed his hands gently on the small of her back, the touch causing a tingling warmth to burst forth within her, flooding her body with need, with wanting, with desperation.

It was what she wanted, too, so why was she hesitating? They'd been about to kiss before they'd been interrupted with the retrieval, so why, now that things were under control, did she hesitate? She didn't know. Sometimes she'd found it better to just jump into the deep end, to sink or swim.

Yes, she knew he would leave her and return to Paris. Yes, she knew he'd broken down far too many of her barriers. Yes, she knew she had to distance herself from him, and the sooner the better, but surely she couldn't deny herself this? This moment? This kiss? This synchronising of their hearts? Hadn't she earned it? All those bad relationships? That pain she'd lived through? Didn't she deserve some sort of reward, even if it was a temporary one?

Breathing in slowly, she held his gaze, ensuring her words and intentions were crystal clear.

'Richard?'

'Mmm?'

'Kiss me,' she whispered. 'Please?'

'You've said that to me once before, Bergan, and we ended up being interrupted by this emergency.' He glanced around at the emergency crews, still doing their job, still needing to continue cleaning up the damage well into the night. The sun was setting but the work would continue, and while he knew the day was far from over for both himself and Bergan, having these few selfish moments would definitely help him recharge his batteries.

'Then you should shut up and get on with it.'

Richard exhaled quickly at her words. 'You never fail to surprise me,' he murmured, his gaze dipping to take in her parted lips, ready, willing and waiting for him.

'Enough talk,' she grumbled impatiently as she laced her fingers into his hair and forced his head down, now almost bursting with need. She was happy that Richard hadn't pushed her, that he'd let her set the pace. She appreciated his chivalry and admired his patience and particularly after they'd been in such a precarious position not too long ago, caring for Wendy and working harmoniously alongside each other. Even she had to admit that enough was enough.

Back in her office, when they'd been standing so close, the need between them so powerful, she could have sworn Richard had been about to kiss her with all the restraint and tenderness he could muster, determined not to scare her, determined to woo her, to show her he cared. Now, though, after everything they'd endured, and with the fact that Bergan herself had very little patience or restraint left, when their mouths finally met, the kiss was hungry, hot and hard.

It was clear that Richard wanted her just as much as she wanted him, and Bergan was unable to fathom how she'd lost control over her desire for him. Here was a man who had been nothing but sweet and considerate to her, especially during the past few weeks. He'd shared his thoughts with her, he'd cuddled her, holding her close and making her feel as though finally she'd found someone she could truly trust.

As his mouth moved over hers, power and passion combined, both of them breathing unsteadily as they allowed themselves to be gathered up in the glorious sensations of a first kiss. While Richard may have felt like he'd waited an eternity for such a moment, his sluggish mind could at least acknowledge that any dreams or thoughts he'd had about kissing Bergan had been seriously underrated. The *real* Bergan was so much better than anything he'd ever contemplated, and his heart swelled with an emotion so huge he was almost too afraid to accept it. Almost…

To realise he was in love with Bergan was one thing, to *tell* her of his feelings was something completely different, especially as they were only just now sharing their first real and honest moment together.

He loved Bergan! Could it be possible? The realisation brought with it a thousand more questions, but, he decided, there was plenty of time for internalisation, and right now he wanted to concentrate on savouring every moment of her mouth moving perfectly against his own.

There was an uncontrollable need powering through them both, as though they'd been denying themselves for far too long and now that things had built to a frenzy, they were unable to quell it.

He gathered her closer, pressing their bodies close together, wishing they weren't dressed in retrieval overalls, as they were hardly the most romantic of outfits, but at the same time unable to really care.

As his mouth continued to create utter havoc with her senses, Bergan wanted nothing more than for the fire pulsing through them to take its natural course. Richard made her feel so…alive and she couldn't remember *ever* feeling this way.

That realisation should have been enough to scare her, to make her break off the kiss and to push free from his arms, and yet she found herself moaning with pleasure against his lips as she plunged her fingers once more into his hair.

The action caused Richard to slow things down just a fraction, but somehow the intensity kept building.

The hunger was still there, but now his lips were more tender. Her heart rate continued to increase, and Bergan was sure that if she'd been hooked up to an ECG machine, she'd have broken it with her off-the-chart heartbeat. She leaned against him, unable to trust her own legs to hold her up. She knew Richard would hold her, that he would ensure she didn't fall—that was the level of trust she had in him—and this time warning bells did start to ring at the back of her mind. She ignored them.

Again and again his perfect and powerful mouth continued to bring forth a surprising and passionate response from her. How was it possible that with a masterful stroke of his tongue, gently caressing her lips, he was able to flood her body with tingles, make her go weak at the knees and cause her mind to stop working? Who was this man? Was he too good to be true?

Another warning bell began to ring, but once again Bergan ignored it.

When he broke his mouth from hers and started pressing a trail of fiery kisses across her cheek and down her neck, nuzzling near her ear, Bergan tilted her head to the side, eagerly allowing him access as she rapidly sucked air into her lungs.

'You are the most stunningly beautiful woman in the world,' he breathed, punctuating his words with little kisses, and she was pleased to note he was just as affected by the kiss as she was. His hands were splayed widely across her back, holding and supporting her, which was something she wanted him to go on doing for ever. Constant, unwavering support.

'For ever?' She whispered the words into the air surrounding them—and instantly wished she hadn't spoken out loud. Then again, it was difficult for her to control her thoughts when her mind had been turned to mush by Richard's masterful touch.

'Sorry?' He pressed more kisses to her neck, wishing her hair was loose, wishing they were somewhere that would afford them a bit more privacy. Although they weren't far from the accident site, Richard had managed to pull her off the main footpath, and now, thanks to the setting sun, they were safe from too many prying eyes, in the shadows of the night.

'Nothing,' she replied, carefully easing her hands from his hair. While he'd been kissing her, she hadn't wanted him to stop—ever. She'd wanted the moment to last for ever, to hear him say the words that would make all her crazy, silly dreams come true. That the two of them could be together...for ever.

Now, though, as her sluggish senses began to return to normal, she was acutely aware of their surroundings, of the number of people still working to clear the rubble, to put up fences and warning beacons to ensure the public's safety.

There were patients to see, a job to do, and she'd been indulging in the desire to finally have Richard's mouth against her own. She could rationalise and give the excuse that they'd been through so much medical trauma tonight they both deserved a few minutes to recharge and regroup, but she didn't like herself when she made excuses. She'd wanted Richard to kiss her. Pure and simple. An opportunity had presented itself and she'd taken it.

He was still bending down, brushing small kisses to her neck and jaw, as though savouring the sensations. Her eyelids fluttered closed as her mind zoomed in on the way his light and feathery kisses were still creating havoc with her equilibrium.

'Do you have any idea what you do to me?'

'Richard,' she breathed again, knowing she needed to put a stop to this. She slid her arms down from his neck, bringing them to rest at the top of his firm chest. 'We need to—'

'I'm so glad we waited until you were ready because I have to tell you, Bergan, I was not disappointed.'

She eased back a little. 'You weren't?' Why did she feel such an overwhelming sense of relief at this news? How was it he always seemed to know just what to say? In the back of her mind, while conscious they needed to stop what they were doing and concentrate on work, she had been wondering what he might be thinking, whether or not the kiss had meant as much to him as it had to her. The fact it had meant *a lot* to her set off another warning bell.

For now, she looked at the way he was smiling at her. 'No. The real Bergan is one hundred times better than any dreams I've had.'

'You dream about me?'

His smile increased. 'You don't dream about me?' There was a slight teasing note in his voice, and before she could say anything, he bent his head and pressed another firm but long and satisfying kiss to her mouth. 'Your lips are perfect for mine,' he murmured, then shifted his stance, marginally loosening his hold on her. 'And I'd like to request a repeat performance later on, once everything else is under control.'

'And you've finished your shift,' she pointed out, a tight pressure starting to wind itself around her heart. She wanted nothing more than to do as he asked, but at the same time being near Richard was starting to cause her to panic.

'Whatever you say, boss.' With great reluctance Richard dropped his arms and released her, before taking a step back. Bergan was surprised to find she felt both cold and bereft without his touch.

That wasn't right. She'd always been fiercely independent. She'd always been in control of her life, yet being here with Richard, wanting to hold him, kiss him and have him close to her at all times was wrong. It had to be wrong because the last thing she felt right now was in control.

She took a step back, putting some much-needed distance between them, rubbing her hands on her upper arms, trying to shake the sensation of returning to his arms… for ever.

'Are you all right?'

'Me? Sure. I'm fine. As fine as fine can be.' She started talking fast. 'I think we need to get back to work. To check and…to do things and find out what's happening with Wendy and see if we can be of assistance anywhere else.'

'Do you want to head to the hospital?' Richard asked.

'You go ahead.' She took another few steps away from him and jerked her thumb over her shoulder. 'I'm going to go see how things are at the community centre.'

'But Palmer said Sunainah had things under control.'

'I know. I just want to check. She might need a break. To have a coffee or use the bathroom and she might not be able to if no one comes to relieve her. You know how busy a makeshift A and E can be.'

'I do. OK. I'll come with you.' He started to take a few steps towards her but she instantly put her hands up to stop him, making sure she didn't accidentally touch him in the process. She was having a difficult enough time controlling the way his nearness made her feel. Now that she knew how glorious it was to kiss Richard, she wanted to do it all the time.

'No. No. It's better that you go back to the hospital, make sure things are under control in A and E.'

'It won't take long to check the community centre,' he continued, clearly not able to take the hints she was dropping.

'Well, OK, then.' A slight edge came into her voice before she could stop it. 'You go to the community centre and I'll head back to A and E. That's probably the better option given it *is* my A and E department.' She gave a nervous laugh and pointed across the road, where she could see two paramedics finishing up securing their patient before leaving for the hospital. 'I'll hitch a ride with them.'

'Bergan?' Richard reached out, putting both hands on her shoulders. 'What's wrong?'

'Wrong? There's nothing wrong. I'm just trying to be efficient, ensure the patients are getting the best care. There's no point in us staying together, walking side by side like we're doing some sort of ward round.' She was talking faster again, trying not to succumb to the warmth of his hands on her shoulders, of the growing need she had to rest her head against his chest, to draw strength from him.

She didn't need his super-fantastic kindness right now. She didn't need his adorableness winding its way around her. She didn't need those hypnotic blue eyes that had the ability to make her forget anyone and everything as soon as she allowed herself to stare at them for more than a few seconds.

No. What she needed was distance, because even acknowledging she wanted nothing more than to be in his arms, feeling safe and secure, as though nothing bad would ever happen to her again, Bergan knew her childish fantasy would end in despair. It was best she kept herself safe, pull away from him sooner rather than later.

'I think Wendy's retrieval shook you up more than you realised,' he murmured, a small frown creasing his brow as though he really didn't understand her.

Bergan clutched at the excuse, using it willingly, even though she knew it wasn't necessarily true. 'You're probably right. We can only keep the professionalism in place for so long before the reality of the situations we see start to seep into our emotions.'

'Hmm.' He looked into her eyes for a moment. 'OK.' He relented, much to her relief. 'I'll check on how Sunainah is progressing at the community centre and you head back to the hospital.'

'OK.' Without another word she turned and all but sprinted over to the paramedics. 'Mind if I hitch a ride?' she asked, climbing into the back of the ambulance without being invited. 'I can care for the patient.'

'Thanks, Bergan,' they said, and within another few minutes she was on her way back to the hospital, away from Richard. Distance. She needed distance so she could think, to try and understand exactly what was going on between the two of them, because of one thing she was certain—that kiss had changed *everything*.

## CHAPTER ELEVEN

IT WAS THE early hours of the morning before Bergan was able to finally make her way home. It had been a very long day, but she hadn't been able to leave the hospital until Wendy had come out of Theatre.

Bergan had stood by the bed in Recovery, looking at the woman who had been so brave, who had done everything they'd asked as the rescue crews had painstakingly removed rubble in order to get her out. She'd spoken to Wendy's family, explaining just how brave Wendy had been. Now, as she watched Wendy sleep, her body in an induced coma, Bergan knew exactly how her patient must have felt.

Wendy had had physical bricks and mortar closing her in. She herself, on the other hand, seemed to be buried beneath a mound of pain and hurt, repressed memories from her past and the inability to believe she could ever be truly happy.

The fact that Richard had broken down so many of her barriers was enough to cause her great anxiety. He was so wonderful and sweet and sexy and caring and… She sighed and closed her eyes, knowing the simple truth was that she didn't deserve a man like him. After everything she'd done in her past, even though she'd done her best to make amends, did she have the right to expect a man of

Richard's calibre to sweep her off her feet and carry her off into the sunset?

'Hey. Here you are. I've been looking for you.'

She turned at the sound of his soft voice, her heart thumping with pure delight at the sight of him. Why did he have to be so…perfect? He looked at the information on the machines around Wendy's bed, nodding his head, pleased with the results. 'It's a miracle she's alive.'

'Yes.' Richard was standing just behind her, the warmth from his body surrounding her like a comforting blanket. Bergan closed her eyes for a moment, breathing in the scent of him, which always seemed to relax her. Her body tingled at his nearness and once more she found it difficult to concentrate.

At this time of the morning there were a few of the nursing staff around the place, but for the most part, as they stood by Wendy's bed, Bergan was only conscious of the two of them. Whenever Richard was near, it was as though the rest of the world melted away. She wanted to ease back a little, to lean against him, and before tonight she probably would have felt secure in doing that, but now…? Since that life-changing kiss? She just wasn't sure what was happening any more.

He was important to her. She liked him more than she could ever remember liking any man before, but the biggest thing that scared her more than anything was that she trusted him. She'd shared a very intimate and emotional part of her upbringing with him, she'd taken him to the drop-in centre, she'd experienced a moment of dreaded fear when Palmer had first told her that Richard was down in the cavern of rubble. What if something bad had happened to him? Even now, reflecting back, her heart was pierced with a pain she couldn't begin to fully comprehend.

It couldn't possibly be love. She didn't *do* love. Not the

lifelong, happily-ever-after type of love that she'd occasionally witnessed. Mackenzie and her new husband John. Even Richard's parents, Helen and Thomas. It was clear that pure love *did* exist…but not for her.

As they stood there, Richard moved closer and draped his arm naturally around her shoulders. For the past few weeks, feeling his gentle, caring touch like this had filled her with delight, had helped her to let go of her stress, had relaxed her, but now, after the kiss, she wasn't sure what his touch meant.

Did it mean he wanted to leave and go somewhere else so they could continue kissing? Would he want *more* than kissing? When she'd been in his arms, she'd most certainly wanted to share more with him, but now…she wasn't so sure. It was as though he'd turned her world upside down and the sensation of falling, of ending up in a bottomless abyss, was enough to make her panic.

'You're so stiff and tense,' he murmured, and shifted behind her, resting both hands on her shoulders before tenderly massaging her trapezius. 'So tight, but I guess after the night we've had both at the retrieval site and in A and E, that's to be expected.' His words, his small chuckle, the warm breath on the back of her neck, the feel of his clever hands kneading away her stress made her feel light-headed. Bergan closed her eyes again, momentarily allowing him access to her, but the pain in her heart, the anxiety pulsing through her body would not be stilled.

'Uh…' She wriggled her shoulders and shifted away from him.

'Are you all right?' He instantly dropped his hands, looking at her quizzically.

'Uh…sure. Just tired and, well, you know, if you keep doing that, I might fall into a puddle at your feet.'

His smile was instant. 'Never mind. I'd pick you up and carry you home.'

Bergan sighed heavily and shook her head. 'Stop being so nice,' she whispered harshly, and then, seeing the surprised confusion in his eyes, she shook her head and walked away. She could almost feel him watching her, wondering what on earth he'd done wrong. Guilt swamped her. She shouldn't have snapped at him but…but… Her mind was spinning and she was unable to think straight, unable to put things into a neat and clear order.

Bergan stopped by her office, gathered what she needed, locked the door and headed to the car park, barely speaking to the security guard who walked her to her car. Driving home, she refused to think about anything except the small amount of traffic on the road. She found a radio station with a late-night talk show, glad of the mindless chatter in the background. It was far easier to listen to people debating the right amount of fertiliser to put on their vegetables in order to achieve award-winning status at local fairs than try and dissect the way she was feeling.

When she arrived home, she put all thoughts of Richard into a box and shoved it into the far recesses of her mind, before going through the motions of getting ready for bed. She was exhausted and yet, as she lay in her bed, tossing and turning and trying to get comfortable, the image of Richard, staring at her as though she'd just punched him in the solar plexus, refused to wipe itself from her memory.

She didn't want to hurt him, but she feared, in her quest for self-preservation, that she must. The sooner she broke things off with him, the less painful it would be. The fact that a connection had developed at all was her fault and she took complete responsibility for any fallout. Richard only had one more week here and then he would leave. Back to Paris. Back to his normal life…his normal life without her.

She pursed her lips at the thought, unable to stop her throat from thickening with sadness, unable to stop tears from springing to her eyes, unable to stop the pain piercing her heart. Richard would leave and he would forget about her. Once again she'd be alone, because that's the way it was supposed to be.

Turning her face into the pillow, Bergan began to weep. She curled into the foetal position, pulling the sheet tight around her as she allowed the pain and loss of the man who meant so much to her to bubble to the surface and overflow in a river of misery.

'Hi, Mum,' Richard said, answering his phone and lying back on the bed. It was his last day in Australia and he was avoiding getting out of bed, following the irrational theory that if he didn't get up, the day wouldn't start. Neither was he in the mood for chatting to his mother. There was only one person he wanted to talk to and *she* had been ignoring him.

In the days following the building collapse Bergan had put the brakes on and had made every effort to make herself completely unavailable to him. Every time he'd called to see when they were next going to get together, she'd make an excuse. He'd sent her text messages and not received an answer until the next day. She'd even gone as far as to change the roster at work, ensuring their shifts didn't overlap.

'All ready to head back to the northern hemisphere?' Helen asked.

'Sure.'

'Richard? You don't sound all that excited. I'd have thought, after travelling for such a long time, you'd be eager to get home.'

'I am, Mum. So, tell me about what you and Dad have

been doing over the past few days,' he said, eager to change the subject, but it appeared Helen was having none of it.

'What's happened?' she asked.

'Nothing, Mum. Everything's fine.'

'Richard, I'm your mother. I know every tone in your voice. Now, I don't expect you to blurt everything out to me, you're a very private man, but I also won't have you insult my intelligence by lying to me when everything clearly isn't fine.'

'I have some things to sort through.'

'Regarding Bergan?'

Richard frowned at the phone. 'How do you figure that?'

Helen chuckled. 'I know every tone in your voice, remember. You may not have spoken much about her directly, but her name has come up quite a bit during our chats. It's not what you say but how you say it, darling.'

'I don't want to talk about it.'

'Mmm-hmm?'

Richard closed his eyes and shook his head. 'She's frustrating, Mum.'

'Mmm-hmm?'

'And annoying and exacerbating. She's driving me insane.'

'Mmm-hmm?'

'We only have a limited amount of time together and over the last few days she's withdrawn from me, not taking my calls, not responding to my emails or text messages. I even wrote her a note and put it in her letterbox. Nothing. I'm leaving the country tonight, returning to Paris, and yet she hasn't wanted to spend time with me and we were… we were so good together. Or maybe it was only me who thought that.'

'Mmm-hmm?'

'Is she upset because I'm leaving? Is that it? If it is, it's ridiculous. She's known from the start that my time in Australia was limited, that I needed to return to Paris to present my findings.'

'Mmm-hmm?'

'Sure, in the beginning I wasn't sure what might happen when I returned to Paris, but that was before we kissed and now… I don't know how it's possible that a kiss can change things but it can—it did. We're perfect for each other and she was the one who showed me it was OK to take a chance, to try again. She's been knocked down so many times in her life, one thing after another, after another, after another and yet she always finds a way to get back on her feet, to persevere, to keep moving forward. She made me realise it was OK to hope again, to know that time would heal wounds and that I'd be able to love again. And I do. I love her but I know if I tell her, she'll run a mile.'

'Mmm-hmm?'

'Or has she already realised that I love her?' Richard opened his eyes and sat up in bed, this new realisation dawning on him. 'Is that why she's run? Perhaps she's realised that my feelings for her are intense and I'll bet hers are equally as intense and that's why she's put the brakes on. She doesn't *want* me to love her because she doesn't know if she can give me love in return.

'Maybe she's worried that when I return to Paris, I'll forget her. Not a chance of that happening. My heart beats out her name.' He shook his head.

'Mmm-hmm?'

'She's stubborn enough to believe that. Stubborn enough to lock herself away, ensuring she doesn't get hurt, and who can blame her, especially after everything she's been through? She doesn't know how to lean on others, how to believe they'll always be there for her. Doesn't she realise that my life is meaningless without her? Doesn't she know that it doesn't matter where I might be living, I'll only be half a person if she's not right there beside me?'

'Mmm-hmm?'

Richard was silent for a moment as everything he'd just been saying started sinking into some form of coherence in his mind. 'I need to speak to her.'

'Mmm-hmm?'

'But she's just finishing the night shift. She'll be tired and then sleeping. Oh, and I have that dinner tonight and as I'm the guest of honour, I have to go.' He growled in frustration. 'I'll leave early. Bergan is more important than any dinner. She's more important than the fellowship, more important than everything.'

'Mmm-hmm.'

'Thanks, Mum. It was great talking to you, but I've got to go. I've got a bit of planning to do.'

'Anytime, darling,' Helen chuckled.

Some of the A and E staff had organised a little farewell dinner for Richard. Bergan had declined to attend, preferring to head home to a quiet night of not thinking about him, knowing she didn't need to fear him casually dropping in.

When a loud knock came from her front door, Bergan almost jumped right out of her skin, gasping in surprise.

'Bergan?' Mackenzie's voice came from the other side of the door. 'Open up or I'll go and get my spare key.'

'I'm coming. I'm coming.' Bergan hurried to the door, checking first that her friend was alone before opening it.

'Hey. I thought you might have been at the dinner for Richard.'

'I was. He looks terrible.'

'He does?' Concern instantly flooded through her. 'Why? What's wrong?'

'You. You're what's wrong.' Mackenzie stormed into the house and turned to glare at her.

'What have I done now?' Bergan asked as she closed the front door then headed into the kitchen, knowing Mackenzie would follow.

'You know exactly what you've done. Why are you pushing Richard away?'

'What? He's leaving tonight. That's hardly pushing him away. The man has to return to Paris—to his *life* in Paris—and that's the end of it.'

'Is it? So...what? You've decided to push him away first? Self-preservation? You're an idiot.' Mackenzie was working herself up into a right rage. 'All those years you told me that if we worked hard, if we just believed, we could change our future. I believed you and *voilà*!' Mackenzie spread her arms wide. 'Look at me now. I'm *happy.* It wasn't always plain sailing, but from my first marriage came Ruthie and now I have John. It does happen, Bergan. Happiness *can* happen for people like us.'

'No. It happens for people like *you.*' Bergan walked to the fridge and opened it, stared inside for a moment before closing the door and turning to face her friend. 'I'm not meant to be happy.'

'Wha—?' Mackenzie stared at her, completely stunned. Bergan stood there, waiting for one of Mackenzie's optimistic tirades, but it didn't come. Instead, Mackenzie just shook her head, turned and walked to the front door. Bergan frowned. Mackenzie was walking out on her? That wasn't how things usually went.

She waited a moment, listening carefully, and when she heard the front door open, she rushed from the kitchen. 'Kenz! Wai—' She stopped when she saw Richard standing in the open doorway, Mackenzie pushing past him.

'Good luck.'

Had she just heard Mackenzie say that softly to Richard? Bergan's gaze took in the sight of the man of her dreams, standing before her. Her knees began to shake, her hands began to tremble and as she glanced at Mackenzie's retreating form, Bergan felt a surge of anger pulse through her. She wasn't sure whether she was more angry that after one look at Richard her body had betrayed her or that Mackenzie had been the betrayer.

'Did you set this up with her?' She stabbed a finger in the direction Mackenzie had gone.

Richard calmly came into her home, closing the door behind him, his voice quiet and controlled. 'You've been avoiding me, Bergan. I'm a desperate man and that means I needed to take desperate measures.'

She shook her head and turned on her heel, heading back into the kitchen. All she needed were a few seconds to regroup, to adjust to him being here, in her home, especially when she'd resigned herself to never seeing him face-to-face again.

When he sauntered casually into the kitchen, leaning against the doorjamb, his thumbs hooked into the back pockets of his jeans, Bergan's heart turned over. Didn't the man have any idea just how handsome he was? How sexy she found him? How she wanted nothing more than to throw herself into his arms and beg him to never let her go? She swallowed over the sudden dryness of her throat.

She shifted around to the other side of the kitchen table. The more obstacles they had between them the better. As she watched him, she realised he wasn't at all agitated, that he was cool, calm and collected. She tried to mimic his calmness and forced herself to cross to the sink and fill the kettle. 'Cup of tea?'

'Sure. Sounds great.'

So that was it? They were just going to chat politely

to each other, drink tea and say goodbye? Was that all he wanted? Feeling as though she'd just had the rug pulled from under her, Bergan wasn't sure what was going to happen next. She took two cups from the cupboard and two teabags.

'How was the dinner?' When he didn't immediately answer, she turned and looked at him over her shoulder.

'I left early.'

Silence floated in the air between them, and from his relaxed, unhurried manner it was clear he wasn't going to make any effort to fill it.

'Oh? But you were the guest of honour.'

'I know.'

'Has that happened often at other hospitals you've visited? That you go out to dinner at the end of your placement?'

Another pause, then a shrug. 'Some.'

Bergan checked the kettle again, wishing it would hurry up and boil, thereby giving her something to do. She leaned against the kitchen cupboards and looked across at him, the uncomfortable tension mounting with each passing second.

'Good to see Wendy doing well.'

Richard nodded.

'Mackenzie said they had to amputate the right leg below the knee but have managed to save the other one.'

He nodded again.

'And Reggie said the bladder and intestinal ruptures are healing nicely.'

'So I've heard.'

Unable to take it any longer, Bergan spread her arms wide. 'What do you want, Richard?'

He raised his eyebrows and a slow smile began to sneak its way across his perfect mouth. 'That's a loaded question, especially coming from you.'

'Why?'

'Because I want you to marry me.' The words were delivered matter-of-factly and Bergan was relieved she was neither drinking nor holding anything in her hands because at those words her mind and body went completely numb.

Eventually, she managed to blink one long blink before staring at him and swallowing. 'M-m-marry?'

'Yes.' It was only then he slowly made his way around to where she was. Bergan felt like a deer caught in a car's headlights, unable to move or look away from this glorious, wonderful, scary man.

'This isn't the official proposal,' he said, coming to stand right next to her, invading her personal space and not seeming to care. 'When I propose, you'll know about it.'

'P-propose?'

His gorgeous smile was heart pounding and mind numbing at the same time. Richard placed his hands on her shoulders and looked down into her eyes. 'I'm in love with you, Bergan, and I have the sneakiest suspicion that you're in love with me.'

'Love?'

'And no doubt that scares the life out of you, which is why you've been incommunicado recently. I understand that, and I'm not going to rush you.'

'You're not?'

He shook his head. 'I'm flying out in a few hours' time and I wanted to spend as much of that time with you as I can.'

'Er…' The concern in her eyes matched the fear pulsing through her. What did that mean? What was she supposed to do? Say? She had wondered whether Richard might try and see her before he left, but she'd half expected him to be as mad as anything.

This calm acceptance of the situation wasn't what she'd

mentally prepared for. She almost wished he'd yell at her, demand reasons why she'd shut him out, but perhaps…just perhaps he knew her better than she'd realised. If he pushed her, she'd get angry, making it easier for her to hate him and to walk away. Ooh, he was clever.

'I don't mind if we just snuggle up on the lounge, watch a bad movie, drink tea, eat popcorn, play a game of Scrabble.' He bent his head and brushed a small kiss on her cheek. 'I just want to be with you, Bergan.'

'Because you…lo—' She stopped and swallowed over the word.

'Love you?' He nodded. 'Yes.'

'And this…declaration isn't supposed to pressure me?'

'That wasn't my intention. I have two weeks of presenting my findings on the fellowship and then you'll fly to Paris to meet me.'

'I will?' The ground shifted beneath her feet yet again. There was disbelief in her tone and finally she started to regain some control over her mind and body. The kettle had switched itself off and as she stepped back Richard dropped his hands, watching as she poured boiling water into the cups. 'I thought you said you weren't going to rush me.'

'I'm also not completely stupid,' he returned. 'Besides, it's not rushing you, Bergan, it's more like giving you a gentle nudge in the right direction.'

'So I'm expected to take time off work away from my busy A and E department and fly off to Paris with barely a moment's notice.'

'Yes.'

'And who will look after A and E?'

'Mackenzie said she'd help organise that.'

'Oh, she did, did she? What else has Mackenzie volunteered for?'

Richard thought for a moment then shook his head.

'Nothing. Reggie is the one who's offered to pick you up and take you to the airport. I've given her the information for the flights that have been booked for you.'

'What?'

'I told you, Bergan. Desperate times call for desperate measures.'

'What about my home? My plants?'

'Mackenzie's daughter Ruthie has agreed to water them for you.'

'And Sunainah? What's her role in all this?' Bergan clattered the spoon roughly from side to side in the teacup, not caring what sort of noise she was making. Had her friends really agreed to gang up on her like this?

'She's going to be keeping you calm.' Richard watched as she threw the teaspoon into the sink then gripped the edge of the bench as she processed everything he was saying.

'So, because I haven't spoken to you all week long, you've turned my friends against me?'

'They love you, Bergan. You know that. They only want what's best for you.'

'Oh, and I suppose that's you?' She shook her head then turned and walked into the lounge room, not caring about the tea.

Richard instantly followed her and placed his arms around her, his chest pressed to her back. 'Yes, as a matter of fact it is. Bergan, I know this is difficult for you, but I can't let you go. You've brought brightness and sunshine back into my life. I love you.'

'And you're OK with that? With just forgetting your life with Chantelle and moving on?'

'I can't live in the past. I can't bring Chantelle back. She knew that. She told me that I needed to move forward and one day find someone else. And that someone else is you,

Bergan. You are unique and kind and a little bit crazy, as well as passionate and faithful. And while, at times, you completely flabbergast and exasperate me, it doesn't change the fact that I am in love with you.'

'And how did you come to this conclusion, then?'

'When you started avoiding me, it made me really stop and think, really take stock of what was going on in my life. This past year, on the fellowship, my life hasn't been normal, and I honestly thought I needed to return to Paris, to finish the fellowship, to figure out who I was after a year of travelling, of having new experiences, and that's why I couldn't give you an answer whenever you asked me what might happen next between us.

'I knew you made me happy, happier than I've been in a very long time, but I wasn't sure how I'd feel when I returned to Europe.'

'And you do now?' She eased away. 'How can you possibly predict what might happen when you return? You can't. This…' she indicated the space between them '…thing between us is nothing more than some sort of holiday romance. When you get back and reality starts to seep into the imaginary world you've been living in, you'll see there's no room for me, no room for a woman with too much baggage to fit into your world.' She shook her head. 'We're better off apart, Richard.'

'Respectfully, Bergan, I completely disagree.'

'How, Richard?' She threw her arms up in the air, her control snapping. 'How can you possibly know that what we have here is something that can last for ever?'

'Because you frustrate me, because you drive me insane, because you perplex me.'

'Thanks a lot.' There was pain in her voice and she could feel tears starting to prick her eyes.

'You also excite me, challenge me, believe in me. My desire to be with you for the rest of my life isn't some whim, Bergan, and when I realised that, I knew it didn't matter whether I was in Paris or Australia or Timbuktu. Wherever I was, I didn't want to be without *you*.'

He closed the distance between them, slipped his arms around her waist and dipped his head to press his lips to hers, all in one swift movement. Anything she might have said disappeared into thin air as all she could focus on was the fact that Richard was kissing her. For days she had craved this, often waking up at night longing for his touch.

Unable to remain strong when he held her like this, when he created such havoc with her senses, she sighed into the embrace, leaning into him, showing him that although she was trying to push him away, she really wanted him as close as possible.

'Bergan,' he eventually said, drawing back slightly, 'you know me better than anyone else. I don't usually talk about Chantelle—to anyone. Of course my parents and my sisters supported me at the time of her death but grief has its own schedule, taking its sweet time to unravel. And that's exactly what I might have done had I not met you. I'd bottled my emotions up for so long, showing the world that I was coping just fine. I accepted the fellowship for two reasons. First, to force myself out of the life I'd boxed myself into. You know, home then hospital, home then hospital day after day after day.'

'Monotonous and lonely,' she stated, listening intently to every word he was saying and unable to stop her heart from being desperately affected by his words.

'Exactly. Second, I knew that when I was travelling, meeting new people, having to give lectures as well as working in different A and E departments in different countries, I could continue to hide, continue to portray that I really was OK.'

'But you weren't?'

'No, and I didn't realise I wasn't, not until I saw you at the Moon Lantern festival.'

'Really?'

'I looked across a crowd of thousands into your eyes and somehow felt as though I'd found my home.' He smiled in bemusement and shook his head. 'It sounds silly to say it out loud, but that's the way it was. I couldn't get you out of my mind, and then when I saw you at the hospital and found out you were not only my hospital contact but also my neighbour, I couldn't believe it. It's as though everything I'd been through in my life had been leading me towards meeting you, towards the time we've shared together, towards asking you to spend the rest of your life with me.'

Bergan started trembling again at his words. 'Is...*that* the propos—?'

'No. Again, you'll know when I'm properly proposing, but I want you to know my intentions are honourable. Old-fashioned, yes, but it's the truth. I love you, Bergan. Nothing will change that.'

She looked away as he said the words, unable to believe how vulnerable hearing them made her feel. Richard loved her. Could that be true? Richard wanted to marry her, to be with her for ever, to live the rest of his life with her. Was she really that worthy?

'Anyway, my real intention for coming here tonight was so I could spend the rest of the time I have in Australia with you.'

Bergan nodded, not trusting her voice because she was so choked up with emotion. Never had anyone made her feel so honoured, so cherished, so loved. Was it really possible for her to have a normal, happy relationship? Mackenzie seemed to think so, and so did Richard. He'd been through so much himself, grieving for his wife, battling loneliness, and yet here he was, standing before her, confessing his feelings, desperate to spend time with her.

Her heart turned over with love, and even though her first inclination was to discount the emotion, telling herself she didn't *do* love, she knew it was a lie. She couldn't, however, admit that to Richard, not yet. The fact that he'd come here to confess his feelings was all that was holding her together, knowing that *he* thought she was worthy of his love. If he'd left, returning to Paris without a word, as she'd expected, given her behaviour over the past few days, then anything he'd confessed wouldn't have had much impact.

He'd blown off his going-away dinner, leaving early even though he was the guest of honour, to come here and spend time with her. *With her!* He'd opened his heart, declared his intentions and was *showing* her exactly how he felt.

Until a few hours ago, she'd accepted her future existence: a life without Richard. Now, though, there were too many different possibilities that flooded through her mind, but in all of them she could picture him by her side, affirming her, encouraging her, believing in her.

With great reluctance he eased his hold on her and led her into the lounge, where they snuggled together, watching a movie and talking quietly as though this was an ordinary 'date' night rather than their last few hours together.

When it was time for him to leave, Richard held her tight in the circle of his arms before dipping his head and pressing slow, soft and sensual kisses to her mouth.

'I don't want you to go,' she whispered in his ear, her voice breaking, as she hugged him close. And when he finally released her, holding her hand until it was necessary to finally let go, he smiled and winked at her.

'That's a very good beginning.'

# CHAPTER TWELVE

'YOU'RE JITTERY.' DRAK sauntered over to where she was sitting at the desk in the drop-in centre.

'Hmm? Pardon?' Bergan looked up from where she'd been reading a document, the pen in her hand being tapped repeatedly on the desktop. Drak glanced pointedly at the pen and it was only then that Bergan seemed to realise she was moving it. 'Sorry.'

'Missing Richard?'

Bergan closed her eyes for a moment and shook her head. 'Not you, too. I get enough hounding from Mackenzie, Sunainah and Reggie.'

'Fine.' Drak held up his hands in surrender. 'I won't mention him.'

'I'd appreciate it.' She'd half expected Drak to walk away, to go and do something else—at least, that's what the *old* Drak would have done. This new Drak, the one who had changed into a responsible adult, pulled up a chair and sat down beside her.

'Whatcha working on?'

'Calendar of events for next year.'

'Need some ideas?'

'Sure. Fire away.' Anything to take her mind off her next big adventure.

Drak came up with several great suggestions and some

not so great. Some were far too silly and way out there to be considered, but they certainly made them both laugh.

'It's good to see you laughing. Haven't seen much of it these past few weeks.'

'No.'

'A lot on your mind, eh?'

She levelled a glare at him. 'Who's been talking to you?'

'Mackenzie. Sunainah. Reggie.'

'They shouldn't have. The last thing you need is to be burdened with my problems.'

'It's not a burden for true friends to be concerned about each other,' he pointed out. 'Besides, the three of them have been to visit Jammo in the rehab clinic, just like you. Jammo's so amazed at how much people *really* care about her.'

'She's a special girl.'

'You don't need to tell me.' Drak shook his head. 'That night…I think I aged a lifetime.'

Bergan smiled. 'Richard and I couldn't believe the way we literally watched you become a man.'

Drak rolled his eyes. 'Hey, don't get all mushy on me, OK? And speaking of Richard—'

'We weren't,' she interrupted, but he ignored her.

'Aren't you supposed to fly to Paris tomorrow?'

'Yes.'

'Are you going?'

'I don't know.'

'Why not?'

Bergan sighed then looked at him. 'Because I'm scared.' She spread her hands wide, not giving him the chance to say anything. 'You know my story. You know how difficult it is for people like us to trust again.'

'But you *do* trust Richard, don't you?'

'Yes.'

'Do you love him?'

Bergan sighed again, thinking of the video calls she'd shared with Richard during the past fortnight, how her heart rate had pounded out such an erratic rhythm the instant she'd seen his face on the screen and how her spirits had plummeted once it was all over.

She felt as though she was living from call to call and she could accept that, but to get on a plane to fly halfway around the world for a *man*? That was something she'd thought she'd never do. Yes, she trusted him. Yes, she loved him, at least she could admit that much now, but in getting on that plane tomorrow, wasn't that a declaration that she was willing to give up her inner self? To share the rest of her life with Richard, knowing he would always be there for her? That she would be there for him? That together they could really start making a different in this world?

'Do you love him?' Drak repeated.

'Yes.' There was a hint of annoyance in her tone at being pushed.

'Then what are you waiting for? Trusting and loving—those are the big things. Oh, and communicating. Jammo and I are working on that now. Making sure we talk to each other, tell each other when we're freaked out and stuff.'

'I'm really happy for you, Drak. I can't believe how only a few weeks ago you didn't want to carry that lantern.'

He laughed at the memory as he rubbed his fingers over a coffee stain on the wall next to him. 'How did you put up with me?'

She laughed back, teasing him. 'I have no idea!'

The smile slowly slid from Drak's face. 'You'll regret it if you don't go.'

'Yeah. I know. It's just…when I'm with Richard, everything is…magnified. I don't know how or why but it just is. Emotions are more powerful, time more precious, happiness more than I could ever imagine.'

'But?' he prompted.

'But what if I lose myself?'

Drak laughed, then quickly sobered. 'Oh, you're not joking. Bergan, I don't think you could ever lose the true person inside you. You're too strong for that.' He pointed to a coffee stain on the wall, one that had been there for as long as Bergan could remember. 'I've looked at this stain so many times over the years. I don't know who spilt their coffee one day but so many times, when I've just zoned out from what's been going on around me, I'd imagine being able to pick up a pen and turn this stain into a beautiful drawing.'

Bergan handed him a pen. 'Show me.'

Drak stared at her for a moment as though she'd lost her marbles, then took the pen from her. Within a matter of a few strokes his natural creativity had managed to change what had been splatters and splotches into two people riding on horses, side by side, off into the sunset. 'Perspective, Bergan. You taught me that. It's how you look at things and what you do with that knowledge that counts.'

Bergan stared at the beautiful drawing on the wall and was surprised when tears pricked her eyes. How could she not have realised how simple it all was? Yes, she considered she had a large stain on her life, but if she added Richard's love to that stain, she could change it into something beautiful.

'I'm going to Paris.' She whispered the words, as though testing them out. She breathed in a deep, cleansing breath. 'I'm going to Paris.' She met Drak's gaze. He just rolled his eyes, but she could see he was trying hard not to smile, still needing to protect his 'tough guy' image. A grin touched her lips and she sat up a little straighter in her chair, thinking of seeing Richard face-to-face, being held in his arms, daring to make something new from the stain that was already on her life. The next time she spoke, her voice was filled with wonder, with excitement, with anticipated happiness. *'Je vais à Paris.'*

Drak nodded and stood up. 'Whatever. Just bring me back a croissant.'

Richard stood at airport arrivals, waiting impatiently. He tried not to pace up and down but wasn't all that successful. He tried sitting. He tried leaning. He tried having a coffee but ended up forgetting about it, letting it go cold. He'd arrived much earlier than necessary, just in case her flight time had changed.

He'd received a text message from Reggie saying she'd taken Bergan to the airport. 'She's eager to see you.' That's what the message had said, and since then, during the long twenty-two hours it took to fly from Brisbane to Paris, he'd been a wreck. Bergan was coming to him. A part of him had thought she might back out, but she hadn't. It only highlighted her inner strength, a strength he loved.

Richard checked the arrivals screen again and saw with great relief and delight that her flight had just landed. She was here. She was physically on the same side of the world as him, in the same country, in the same city, in the same airport. The time it took for her to disembark, pick up her luggage and go through immigration seemed to take an eternity but finally—*finally*—she was here.

He hadn't been quite sure what sort of reception he'd receive but what he had not mentally pictured was Bergan opening her arms wide and all but launching herself at him. With a happiness he hadn't thought he could feel, Richard caught her, instantly pressing his mouth to hers in a long-overdue kiss. He couldn't think right now, couldn't worry whether or not he was rushing her, because she was here. *His Bergan* was finally in his arms, her lips pressed against his.

'I've missed you,' she whispered the instant her lips left his.

'Really?' Richard eased her back a little, one arm still firmly around her waist, holding her in a fashion that was clearly possessive.

'Of course. Haven't you missed me, too?'

He swallowed at her words. 'More than you could possibly know.'

Bergan smiled and relaxed. She had two weeks' holiday booked and as it had been quite a while since she'd been to Paris, she was determined to enjoy herself, especially with Richard by her side.

As they headed for the taxi rank, Richard continued to have at least one arm about her, brushing small kisses to her cheeks and neck and lips. Bergan looked into his face and couldn't believe the love that seemed to flow freely from her heart. How...why had she ever tried to deny just how important this man was to her?

'How far is your apartment?' she asked.

'Twenty minutes. Not too bad.'

'Are your parents still here?'

He shook his head. 'They're staying at a hotel tonight and catching a very early train tomorrow morning. They're heading to Wales to see some family friends.'

'Oh. I'm sorry to have missed them.' Bergan smiled to herself as he hailed the taxi, wondering if Helen and Thomas hadn't been evicted from Richard's apartment simply because she was coming.

Richard hailed a taxi and after stowing her luggage in the boot sat with her in the back, his arms firmly around her. He kissed her slowly, carefully, not wanting anything to upset her but at the same time unable to keep his hands or lips off her.

'Don't you have any idea just how addictive you are?'

'Especially after so many weeks apart,' she murmured, equally interested in having his mouth firmly on hers. They were like a couple of teenagers, but neither of them cared, and when they finally arrived at his apartment, Richard insisting on carrying her suitcase up the two flights of stairs, Bergan entered the dark hallway and wandered through into the main living area, gasping in delight at the sight that greeted her.

Tealight candles seemed to be everywhere, their flames flickering perfectly, illuminating the area with a rosy glow.

'Richard?' She reached behind her for his hand but all he did was relieve her of her carry-on luggage. As she continued to look, noticing the mix of red and white rose petals scattered carefully around the furniture, she couldn't help but laugh in astonishment at the tealights on the table, arranged in a heart shape. 'How did you do all this?'

The scents of the candles mixed with the rose petals made a heady combination, and Bergan simply couldn't have removed the large smile from her face, even if someone had asked. She clutched her hands to her chest as she walked slowly and carefully around the place. It had to have been his mother who had set all this up. It was typical of Helen to want to help out, but how had Richard known? Was this as much of a surprise to him as it was to her?

'Richard?' she called again, and this time when she turned to look for him it was to find him holding out a perfect blue rose to her. 'Oh, my!' It wasn't until she reached out to take it from him that she realised her hands were trembling.

'H-how did you know?'

'Reggie. She was very forthcoming about the blue-rose

theory, and I have to say you are unique and more beautiful than any flower, my Bergan.'

'Oh.' She swallowed over the lump that had formed in her throat at his heartfelt words. The instant she took the flower he pulled a small box from his pocket and went down on one knee, holding out his free hand to her.

'Bergan?'

The trembling was getting worse now, spreading from her fingers right through her entire body as she stepped forward and placed her hand in his.

'I told you that when I proposed, you'd know about it.'

'True. Very true.' She looked from him to the beautiful room then back again, gazing down at the man of her dreams, the one man, the most perfect man for her.

'Bergan.'

'Yes, Richard.'

'Will you do me the honour of becoming my wife?'

She bit her lip, her heart pounding so wildly against her ribs it was a wonder she could actually hear him speak. She swallowed once, twice, then smiled at him and nodded. 'Yes. A most definite *yes*.'

'Whew!' He chuckled then leaned forward and pressed a smooth kiss to her hand before opening the box. Inside, nestled on a soft blue velvet cushion, was a perfect pink diamond. 'You can choose the setting and the style of the ring. We'll have it made up.'

'Really?' He was letting her take control.

'Really.' He slowly rose to his feet, watching as she took the box from him, studying the perfectly cut stone.

'Richard. It's…' The enormity of the situation overcame her and to her utter surprise tears gathered behind her eyes. 'It's…perfect.' When she looked up at him, it was to find him staring down at her with the same sort of wonderment.

'You are. Most definitely perfect.' He wrapped his arms

around her and drew her close. 'I love you so much, Bergan. I can't promise that our life together will always be smooth sailing, but I do promise to love and trust you for the rest of my days. We'll talk, we'll laugh, we'll cry and we'll do it *together*.'

'Yes.' She accepted his kisses and sighed against him, occasionally glancing down at the diamond—*her* diamond! 'How *did* you organise all of this? Was it your mother?'

'She lit the candles. I sent her a text when I was stowing your luggage in the taxi.'

'You fiend. And what if I'd been less than enthusiastic when I'd arrived at the airport? Or completely jet-lagged?'

'Then the plan would have changed, but as it was, with the way you all but launched yourself at me—'

'I did not!' she protested hotly as Richard led her to the soft sofa, pulling her onto his lap.

He kissed the tip of her nose. 'I beg to differ, but either way it gave me a clear indication that whatever had been holding you back had been resolved.'

'You gave me these two weeks to figure things out.' She nodded slowly. 'I did and I feel as though an enormous weight has been lifted from my shoulders.' Then she told him about the coffee stain and how Drak had drawn a perfect picture from it.

'Remind me to make Drak a groomsman at our wedding,' Richard said, and Bergan laughed.

'I doubt he'd see having to dress up in some suit as a reward.'

'Perhaps he'd make us a wedding lantern?'

'Good idea. One we can let go and have fly off into the night.'

'On the beach.'

'At dusk.'

'Perfect.' Bergan sighed against him, smiling happily.

'All this wedding talk isn't freaking you out?'

She shook her head. 'Nope. I'm right where I should be. It's been a long time coming but finally…' she snuggled closer, safe and secure in the protective circle of his arms '…I've found my home.'

# EPILOGUE

'BUT WHY?' REGGIE protested.

'I thought you would have been happy to dress up in a pretty pink party dress, Reggie.' Bergan stood in the large white marquee reserved for the bride and her attendants, and smoothed a hand down her very simple, very plain, very elegant white wedding gown, staring at herself in the long mirror, unable to believe the woman looking back was actually her. It had happened. She'd found her Prince Charming and he'd made her the happiest princess on earth.

During the past four months, as Richard had relocated back to Australia and the Sunshine Coast, Bergan's love for him had increased every day. She was so proud, so happy to finally be a bride—a bride with a groom whom she loved and trusted with all her heart.

'I am but it's just…it makes me look about seventeen years old.'

'Oh, woe is you for having such a youthful complexion.' Bergan shook her head, small tendrils of auburn curls floating lightly at her neck, the rest of her hair pulled into a fancy arrangement on top of her head, which had taken the hairdresser almost an hour to achieve.

'Do you like the dress, Aunty Sunainah?' Ruthie, the

experienced flower girl who was wearing a dress identical to those of the rest of the bridesmaids, asked.

'I'll wear whatever it is my friend bids me wear on her wedding day, but I do have to say the style and colour perplexes me slightly.'

'Kenz? Care to explain?' Bergan asked as Mackenzie finished touching up the bride's lipstick.

'On the rare occasions, when we were in foster-care, that things actually were going smoothly, Bergan and I indulged our imaginations in planning her wedding.'

'Not your weddings?' Reggie asked.

Mackenzie shook her head. 'I would change mine almost every time, unable to choose exactly what I wanted, but Bergan had this crazy idea that all bridesmaid's dresses should be pink. Pink party dresses with tulle and lace. Fluffy and puffy.'

'So we're fulfilling a childhood fantasy?' Reggie checked.

'Exactly,' Bergan replied, smooching her lips together to blot the lipstick. Outside the marquee, the string quartet started to play and Ruthie started jumping up and down with excitement.

'It's starting. It's starting!'

'Yes,' Mackenzie told her daughter. 'So get your little basket of flowers and get ready because you go down first, remember.'

'I remember, Mummy,' Ruthie replied, her fingers sifting through the lovely blue rose petals in her basket. 'I have been a flower girl before, you know.'

Mackenzie only grinned at her daughter before turning to look at the blushing bride. 'Ready?'

Bergan smiled at her friend, then, before she picked up her bouquet of blue roses, held out her hands to her friends, Ruthie included. 'Thank you. I don't know what else to say, but without the three of you in my life, and for the last six years beautiful Ruthie as well, I wouldn't be here today. I don't *do* friendships easily, but you've stuck with me through so many different things—especially you, Kenz. So, yeah…' She laughed. 'Thanks.'

'Why do you brides always do this?' Reggie grumbled as she sniffed and blinked rapidly, carefully dabbing at her eyes with a tissue before picking up her bouquet of white roses. 'Why do you say these heartfelt words and then make us all want to cry when you know full well we can't because we'll smudge the make-up that took for ever to apply?'

Bergan laughed and nodded. 'I never thought I would, but then, I never thought I'd find that one true, perfect man for me.'

'But you did, and he's waiting, probably rather impatiently, for you now,' Sunainah said.

'I think Drak's probably more impatient than Richard,' Bergan added. 'Impatient to get out of that suit.' With John, Mackenzie's husband, and Thomas, his father, as his other groomsmen, that only left Helen, Richard's mother, on her own, so Bergan had asked a special favour of her future mother-in-law.

'Ready?' Helen asked, poking her head through the opening of the marquee. 'Oh, Bergan,' she gasped. 'You look breathtaking.'

'No crying!' Reggie demanded, holding out a hand towards Helen.

'Yes. Yes. Of course.' Helen sniffed. 'You're right.' She dragged in a deep breath and held out her hand to Bergan. 'It's time for me, not to give you away as happens to most brides on their wedding day, to walk you down the aisle, *accepting* you into our family.'

'Is it time *now*?' Ruthie demanded, and after everyone

had taken a deep, cleansing breath and as the music rose to a beautiful crescendo, Bergan nodded.

'It's time.' And with the happiest smile on her face she started her walk towards the only man in the world for her—her Richard.

* * * * *

# *Mills & Boon® Hardback*

## *August 2013*

## ROMANCE

| | |
|---|---|
| **The Billionaire's Trophy** | Lynne Graham |
| **Prince of Secrets** | Lucy Monroe |
| **A Royal Without Rules** | Caitlin Crews |
| **A Deal with Di Capua** | Cathy Williams |
| **Imprisoned by a Vow** | Annie West |
| **Duty At What Cost?** | Michelle Conder |
| **The Rings that Bind** | Michelle Smart |
| **An Inheritance of Shame** | Kate Hewitt |
| **Faking It to Making It** | Ally Blake |
| **Girl Least Likely to Marry** | Amy Andrews |
| **The Cowboy She Couldn't Forget** | Patricia Thayer |
| **A Marriage Made in Italy** | Rebecca Winters |
| **Miracle in Bellaroo Creek** | Barbara Hannay |
| **The Courage To Say Yes** | Barbara Wallace |
| **All Bets Are On** | Charlotte Phillips |
| **Last-Minute Bridesmaid** | Nina Harrington |
| **Daring to Date Dr Celebrity** | Emily Forbes |
| **Resisting the New Doc In Town** | Lucy Clark |

## MEDICAL

| | |
|---|---|
| **Miracle on Kaimotu Island** | Marion Lennox |
| **Always the Hero** | Alison Roberts |
| **The Maverick Doctor and Miss Prim** | Scarlet Wilson |
| **About That Night...** | Scarlet Wilson |

0713 GEN STD HB

# ROMANCE

|  |  |
| --- | --- |
| **Master of her Virtue** | Miranda Lee |
| **The Cost of her Innocence** | Jacqueline Baird |
| **A Taste of the Forbidden** | Carole Mortimer |
| **Count Valieri's Prisoner** | Sara Craven |
| **The Merciless Travis Wilde** | Sandra Marton |
| **A Game with One Winner** | Lynn Raye Harris |
| **Heir to a Desert Legacy** | Maisey Yates |
| **Sparks Fly with the Billionaire** | Marion Lennox |
| **A Daddy for Her Sons** | Raye Morgan |
| **Along Came Twins...** | Rebecca Winters |
| **An Accidental Family** | Ami Weaver |

# HISTORICAL

|  |  |
| --- | --- |
| **The Dissolute Duke** | Sophia James |
| **His Unusual Governess** | Anne Herries |
| **An Ideal Husband?** | Michelle Styles |
| **At the Highlander's Mercy** | Terri Brisbin |
| **The Rake to Redeem Her** | Julia Justiss |

# MEDICAL

|  |  |
| --- | --- |
| **The Brooding Doc's Redemption** | Kate Hardy |
| **An Inescapable Temptation** | Scarlet Wilson |
| **Revealing The Real Dr Robinson** | Dianne Drake |
| **The Rebel and Miss Jones** | Annie Claydon |
| **The Son that Changed his Life** | Jennifer Taylor |
| **Swallowbrook's Wedding of the Year** | Abigail Gordon |

0713 GEN STD LP

# *Mills & Boon® Hardback*

## *September 2013*

## ROMANCE

| | |
|---|---|
| **Challenging Dante** | Lynne Graham |
| **Captivated by Her Innocence** | Kim Lawrence |
| **Lost to the Desert Warrior** | Sarah Morgan |
| **His Unexpected Legacy** | Chantelle Shaw |
| **Never Say No to a Caffarelli** | Melanie Milburne |
| **His Ring Is Not Enough** | Maisey Yates |
| **A Reputation to Uphold** | Victoria Parker |
| **A Whisper of Disgrace** | Sharon Kendrick |
| **If You Can't Stand the Heat...** | Joss Wood |
| **Maid of Dishonour** | Heidi Rice |
| **Bound by a Baby** | Kate Hardy |
| **In the Line of Duty** | Ami Weaver |
| **Patchwork Family in the Outback** | Soraya Lane |
| **Stranded with the Tycoon** | Sophie Pembroke |
| **The Rebound Guy** | Fiona Harper |
| **Greek for Beginners** | Jackie Braun |
| **A Child to Heal Their Hearts** | Dianne Drake |
| **Sheltered by Her Top-Notch Boss** | Joanna Neil |

## MEDICAL

| | |
|---|---|
| **The Wife He Never Forgot** | Anne Fraser |
| **The Lone Wolf's Craving** | Tina Beckett |
| **Re-awakening His Shy Nurse** | Annie Claydon |
| **Safe in His Hands** | Amy Ruttan |

0813 GEN STD HB

## ROMANCE

| | |
|---|---|
| **A Rich Man's Whim** | Lynne Graham |
| **A Price Worth Paying?** | Trish Morey |
| **A Touch of Notoriety** | Carole Mortimer |
| **The Secret Casella Baby** | Cathy Williams |
| **Maid for Montero** | Kim Lawrence |
| **Captive in his Castle** | Chantelle Shaw |
| **Heir to a Dark Inheritance** | Maisey Yates |
| **Anything but Vanilla...** | Liz Fielding |
| **A Father for Her Triplets** | Susan Meier |
| **Second Chance with the Rebel** | Cara Colter |
| **First Comes Baby...** | Michelle Douglas |

## HISTORICAL

| | |
|---|---|
| **The Greatest of Sins** | Christine Merrill |
| **Tarnished Amongst the Ton** | Louise Allen |
| **The Beauty Within** | Marguerite Kaye |
| **The Devil Claims a Wife** | Helen Dickson |
| **The Scarred Earl** | Elizabeth Beacon |

## MEDICAL

| | |
|---|---|
| **NYC Angels: Redeeming The Playboy** | Carol Marinelli |
| **NYC Angels: Heiress's Baby Scandal** | Janice Lynn |
| **St Piran's: The Wedding!** | Alison Roberts |
| **Sydney Harbour Hospital: Evie's Bombshell** | Amy Andrews |
| **The Prince Who Charmed Her** | Fiona McArthur |
| **His Hidden American Beauty** | Connie Cox |